MW01515598

Praise for Rida.
Great Love and *The Legacy Tree*:

"Allen is at the top of her game, creating a realistic heroine who is far from just a head on a Popsicle stick. The author takes care in proving that beauty is in the eye of the beholder, and creates a hero who allows his heart to lead him. I enjoyed this witty and heart-touching tale of true love and real life."
Faith V. Smith, *Romantic Times BOOKClub Magazine* review of *Great Love*.

"*[Great Love]* proves that even though you may have the best intentions at heart, people sometimes get hurt. Feelings get bruised, egos tweaked, relationships strained. But Sam and Jonathan will also prove to you that love has no boundaries, no growth chart, no one-size-fits-all mentality. Love comes in all shapes, all sizes; and where there's respect and passion, the size of your heart will always win out over the size of your clothes."
Jennifer Wardrip, RomanceJunkies.com

"*Great Love,* is a delightful book with a heroine to whom many female readers will relate. Well written, with touches of humor, the book is a quick read because it is fast paced. Samantha and Jonathan's humanness is the very essence of the book, making them more real than most characters. Rida Allen delivers a sweet, touching romance between two vulnerable people. Readers will be cheering for Samantha and Jonathan all the way through *Great Love*."
Courtney Bowden, *Romance Reviews Today*

"As the romance blossoms between Jonathan and Samantha, it is evident that Ms. Allen's ability to draw out the characters allows the reader to really get to know two very different individuals who are falling in love. I was sad to see the story end and kept wondering what else might have happened. *Great Love,* is a fantastic romance that will make any night even more special."
Jennifer Bennett, VenusImaging.com.

"[*The Legacy Tree*] is the second novel I have read from Rida Allen, and again I am impressed beyond belief. I typically do not care for contemporary novels, but the work of Rida Allen always has me furiously turning pages to see where the characters will go. I would highly recommend this book, especially for one of those lazy Sundays where you can spend all day reading, because I guarantee you'll finish this in one sitting."
Melissa M. Curran, Scribesworld.com.

"*The Legacy Tree,* is a very sweet love story of two people who are attracted to each other, but who don't really know how to express their feeling to the other. This is a book for a true romantic. I guess that's why I enjoyed it so much that I actually read the whole book twice... Can we say KEEPER? Yes, I will be keeping this book; and I highly recommend it to all readers."
Darlene Howard, Escape to Romance.com.

"*The Legacy Tree,* is a true love story about two people who are right for each other, but need to overcome their own fears and insecurities before they can reach out and grab the love that is waiting for them. It's a story that makes you care about the characters right from the beginning. And it's a story that's unbelievably easy to read, so much so that the time flies right by. And so I find myself, once again, eagerly awaiting the next book to come from author Rida Allen."
JaToya Love, A Romance Review.com.

"Rida Allen tells a beautiful, gentle and heart-wrenching love story that doesn't disappoint and had me hoping that Robyn and Erik would find their way to each other and live happily ever after. [*The Legacy Tree*] is for the romantic at heart, one that I will recommend for a long time to come. Sometimes the greatest loves begin with friendship. Erik's brother George also has his own story. Be sure to read *Truth and Lies,* to see what happens to George and his little girl Jessica. I

am eager for this release!"
Tracey West, *The Road to Romance*.
***

Reviews for *Truth and Lies*:

Rida Allen returns with Truth and Lies, the long-awaited sequel to *The Legacy Tree*. *Truth and Lies*, is George's story (Erik's brother). George's daughter, Jessica, is now two years older. George shows his wonderful father qualities in this tale—I know I was wondering about that when we met George in *The Legacy Tree*. At that time, George, was a new father and feeling very overwhelmed. I was glad to see that in *Truth and Lies*, George still has some doubts about fatherhood, but he stepped up to the plate, and is an amazing father.

Readers are once again swept under with Ms. Allen's heartfelt words, charismatic characters, and family bonds in Truth and Lies. George and Val are both "gun-shy" about love and face many obstacles in their journey together. Their vulnerabilities make them all the more believable. Rida Allen handles her latest sweet and heartwarming contemporary romance masterfully and with heart.

Truth and Lies, is highly recommended from this reviewer!

I am very happy to say that there is a book 3 in the works from Rida Allen in connection with The Legacy Tree and Truth and Lies. Keep checking Rida's site for updates on book 3, The Fashionable P.I., coming soon. Plus, look for book 4 and 5! This reader is looking forward to them all!

Tracey West, *The Road to Romance*
September 2003

Rida Allen's second book, in a series of five connected books, is a wonderful love story of miscommunication and misunderstandings as Val and George struggle their exes. This book has intrigue and mystery, as Val tries to find out about her parents. This book also has plenty of romance. Readers will feel the sexual tension between Val and George.

The author has created wonderful personalities for the characters in this book and they are very believable. The story is not too long or too short and doesn't have any dull moments. This is a well-written book and flows beautifully and isn't a bit choppy. Ms. Allen is a gifted writer and has a winner in *Truth and Lies*.

Ms. Allen's contemporary romance books of full-figured heroines are a delight. How refreshing to read about women of all shapes and sizes finding love. *Truth and Lies*, is a delight to read. This reviewer is anxiously awaiting the release of the next book in the series, *The Fashionable P.I.*, to find out what happens next.

Penny, *Love Romances*
November 2003

Rida Allen has done an exquisite job of bringing life to her characters and this storyline. Not one time while reading Truth and Lies did I have a hard time believing this story. It deals with issues that face real life people everyday. And I absolutely adored the way she made Jessica and family values a very intricate part of the book. It's a perfect modern day romance that I will gladly read again.

Angel, *The Romance Studio*
September 2003

Rida Allen has created another enjoyable tale in *Truth and Lies*. Fans of Robyn and Erik Richards from *The Legacy Tree* will be happy to see them as supporting characters in this follow-up novel. As we learn all about Erik's brother, George, we also get to catch up on the lives of Robyn and Erik. Ms. Allen's storytelling style is both humorous and sensitive, making this latest book a very enjoyable, very satisfying read.

Brooke Wills, *Romance Junkies*
Fall 2003

Truth and Lies

Rida Allen

PublishAmerica

Baltimore

First printing

ISBN: 1-4137-0815-3
PUBLISHED BY PUBLISHAMERICA, LLLP
www.publishamerica.com
Baltimore

Printed in the United States of America

Dedication

This book is dedicated to my husband, Rob, for the support he gives me as I take on my writing career. Thank you, my love, for being my everything.

Also, many thanks to my parents who continue to encourage me as I pursue this career that both delights and frustrates me! And thank you, Dad, for spending money in order to help me make money.

A wholehearted thank you to my brothers, my sister-in-law, and Aunt Fran and Uncle Sy for their love and support.

To my brother, Mike, who is one of my best friends; even if he can't buy all the right computer parts the first time around, I say "tartlets" and "poo-chetta".

To my best friend Heather for her friendship and to my wonderful friend Patty for her bravery in taking on her new life.

Never in doubt, I continue to dedicate my work to my Nana and in memory of my Papa.

And as always, to the dogs! (Sugar, Crystal, Brandi, and our newest addition, Bailey)

Chapter
One

George stretched leisurely in his king-size bed before prying open his eyes. He was met with soft light filtering through the blinds covering his windows. Raking a hand through his short brown hair, he sighed and swung his legs over the side of the bed.

The room was neat and clean, decorated specifically for a man in navy and light gray. The plush carpet under his feet was dark blue and soft to the touch. Wriggling his toes, he was glad he had paid extra for the little luxury. Standing, he rolled his head to loosen his neck muscles, then went into the bathroom.

After a quick shower, he was out and dressed. Without another look at his unmade bed, he left the room. Striding down the hall, he entered what he lovingly called the cotton candy room. It was painted the exact shade of pink cotton candy that you might find at a local carnival. And there she was, huddled on her side underneath a Pepto-Bismol colored blanket.

With a gentle hand, George caressed her fine blond hair. "Jess," She mumbled but did not stir. He wanted to let her sleep but they had a busy day ahead of them. "Jessica, time to get up."

Scrunching up her nose, her eyes opened slightly. "Daddy?"

"Time to get up, sweets," his voice was husky with love. "Go brush your teeth and wash your face."

"Can we have pancakes?" she asked sleepily.

"Not today, baby. I'll make you some cereal and juice. Can you get dressed without me?"

She sniffed and rolled off her bed. "I can do it…I'm not a baby."

"All right. Come down to the kitchen when you're done," he called after her as she disappeared into her bathroom. Shaking his head, he strode downstairs to make his coffee and her breakfast. Had it only been four years since her birth? He wasn't sure he could remember his life as a swinging bachelor before then.

In the kitchen he pulled out a bowl, spoon and milk. After setting those items on the table, he went to the cabinet to see what kind of cereal they had left. Groaning, he saw that they only had raisin bran...he desperately needed to go grocery shopping. He crossed his fingers hoping his daughter wouldn't make a fuss. Instead of leaving the box on the table for her to see, he just poured it in her bowl and tucked it back away in the cabinet. As he was pouring a glass of juice, his little princess scurried into the room. He grunted softly but did not point out that her purple shirt and orange pants did not match. They were her favorite items of clothing and it was her big day.

"Daddy, you poured my cereal!" she frowned at him. "*I* wanted to pour it."

"I'm sorry, sweets. I'll let you pour it tomorrow, okay?"

She pushed out her lower lip but slid onto her chair without any further comment. It took her less than ten minutes to scarf down her food. "I'm done."

"Finish your juice," he ordered, taking a final sip of his coffee before placing the half-full cup in the sink.

She gulped down the remaining juice then stood. "Do I get to use my new backpack today?"

"You bet. It's in the front hall." It was her first day of preschool and she was excited...he was terrified. Up until this point, Jessica had spent her days at home with him or with their part-time nanny, Jennifer. But it was time for Jessica to start socializing with other children. She was ready for the new adventure...he was not.

"Dad-dy!"

He grinned and collected his jacket and briefcase. In the foyer Jessica was hopping from one foot to another, pink backpack perched on her small shoulders. "Okay, lets go." Following her out to the minivan, he groaned out loud. They forgot to do her hair. It was blond, long and straight, which made it easy to deal with. However, if he didn't put it up now, it would end up tangled and riddled with dirt or paint or something. "Jess, we have to put up your hair," he called.

She skipped on, reaching the minivan quickly. "Nah."

"Oh yes we do," he muttered, sliding open the back door. As she clambered into the booster seat, he scrounged in the glove compartment for her extra brush and rubber bands. "Turn your head, sweets."

She obliged as she swung her legs back and forth. "Ouch!" There was hurt in her voice as he pulled the brush through her hair quickly and caught a tangle.

"Sorry," he grunted. When he finished, he tossed the brush back into the glove box and closed her door. Once he was in the car, he turned to look at her. "Jennifer will pick you up this afternoon, okay?"

Nodding, she played with the strap of her backpack. "I'm going to have fun today."

"You sure are," he said confidently, though his heart twinged painfully at the thought of his baby girl going out into the big wide world.

Valerie Adamson cringed as she eyed her bank statement. That was it, she was going to have to sell the house…and the car. Where the hell was she going to live? Selling the house would barely pay off the two mortgages her ex-husband Craig had taken out. Selling her ten year old car would barely give her a small cushion to live on. Darn him.

She uncrossed her legs and got to her feet. The family room she was sitting in was large, longer than it was wide, with a beautiful brick fireplace at the far end. She'd loved this room, though her ex had claimed it was too informal for entertaining. One long wall of the room faced out over the back yard and had multiple windows to let in the afternoon light. She had always envisioned having a nice family evening in this room…a little boy laying on the floor watching TV, a little girl playing with her dolls on the couch. Instead she and her ex had spent most of their time entertaining in the more formal living room at the front of the house. It was more square with windows on two walls and french doors to a dark-paneled den on the third wall.

With a grunt of disgust, she carried her papers into the kitchen where boxes of her files were lined up on the floor. All the furniture

11

in the house was already gone...repossessed...so at least moving would be a snap. She dropped the latest bank statement into a box and continued on to her refrigerator. The kitchen was spotless, as always, and styled after an old-fashioned country-kitchen. There was a bay window that overlooked the manicured back yard and an island in the center of the kitchen itself. This, too, had been a favorite room, with it's cozy breakfast nook and oak cabinets. The appliances were not new, but were clean and in excellent condition. She'd spent many a time here preparing meals and cocktails for their dinner parties, preferring her own cooking over any catering company's food. And her ex had approved, stating that his clients would find it "quaint" that his wife liked to cook for their guests.

Staring into the fridge, she chewed on her lip. The shelves were practically empty, which was a far cry from previous months. She had always made sure the pantry and refrigerator were full of home-cooked goodies in case any clients or friends dropped by. But now, now it was different. There were no more clients, no more entertaining friends on a Friday night. There was just her...and her non-existent budget. Slamming the door shut, she turned to the pantry. Yech...peanut butter and jelly again.

After making herself a sandwich, she grabbed the newspaper to search for a job...an apartment...a new life.

George groaned and dropped into his kitchen chair.

"I am so sorry," Jennifer said, rinsing a dish in the sink. "Roger's company isn't moving us until next month so at least I'll be here a little while longer."

"Jessica is going to be heartbroken. You've been with us for so long!" he told her.

"And I love her to death," Jennifer whispered. "But this is Roger's big opportunity."

He patted her shoulder as he passed her to leave the room. "I don't know what we're doing to do without you."

"I'll ask around and see if anyone is interested in the job," she offered.

"We appreciate that," he responded before leaving the room. Jennifer was leaving! What was he going to do? All those horrible interviews and frightening thoughts of the applicant's backgrounds. Jennifer had been a true find...a diamond in a mountain of coal. Walking into the family room, he saw his precious daughter sprawled on the floor coloring a picture. "What are you drawing, baby?"

"A picture for class," she answered absently.

He sat on the edge of the couch and sighed, "Sweets, Daddy needs to talk to you for a minute."

"Okay," she dropped her crayons and hopped over to him. "Hi!" she chirped, kissing his cheek.

Hugging her against him, he saw Jennifer appear in the archway. "Honey, Jennifer is going to be leaving us."

"I know, Daddy...she leaves every day," Jessica said logically.

"You're right," he confirmed. "But what I was trying to say was that Jennifer will be moving away with her husband."

She frowned. "Moving away?"

"They're moving to Washington, D.C. You remember that Uncle Erik, Aunt Robyn and Maddie live far away? That's where Jennifer is going." He was trying to simplify where Jennifer was moving by bringing up his brother and sister-in-law's location in Maryland. They had visited Erik and Robyn dozens of times since they had gotten married.

Jessica heard only one thing. "Far away?" her voice trembled with tears.

At that point, Jennifer entered the room and knelt next to the little girl. "I'll come back and visit. We'll talk on the telephone and I'll send you letters that your daddy can read to you."

The lower lip came out and big fat tears began rolling down Jessica's cheeks. "I don't want you to go far away!" Throwing her arms around Jennifer's neck, she hung on. "I'll be good! Please don't go!"

George groaned and placed a big hand on his daughter's little head. How do you explain something like this to a child whose world was so small? She had him, she had her grandparents nearby, and then she had Jennifer for the past two years.

"Babe, I'm not leaving because you were bad!" Jennifer told her softly. "I'm going to miss you, but I have to go away with Roger."

Jessica cried harder and pressed her face into her caregiver's neck. "Don't leave me!"

Jennifer looked up at George for help.

He picked up his daughter and held her in his lap. "Sweets, Jennifer isn't leaving for a few weeks, so we can talk about this again, okay? She'll be back tomorrow and we'll figure out how we can stay in touch with her after she moves away."

With a sigh, Jennifer stood and kissed Jessica's head. "We'll talk again tomorrow, babe."

Jessica continued to sob against her father's chest as Jennifer left the house.

"C'mon now, Jess. We want Jennifer to be happy, right?"

She nodded against him, hiccuping tearfully.

"She's happy to be going away with her husband, Roger. She'll be sad to leave you, but happy to start a new life. So do you know what we should do?"

"What?" she whispered.

"We should make her some pictures to take with her," he said, kissing her temple. "Okay?"

Sniffling, she nodded.

"Okay, you get started and I'll go make hot dogs for dinner."

Her eyes brightened and she slid to the floor. Biting her lip, she grabbed a crayon and a clean sheet of paper.

George stood and strode back into the kitchen. At four years old, hot dogs solve almost anything...he only wished it were that easy for this thirty-two year old.

Valerie sat cross-legged on the floor, playing with her best friend's daughter, Madelyn.

"So, what are you going to do?" Robyn Richards asked from her place on the couch.

Val laughed as Maddie raced around the coffee table, her short brown curls bouncing against her head, to hug her dog, Jasmine. "Sell. I'll sell the house and the car and pray for some kind of job with room and board."

"What can you do that would have room and board?"

Valerie looked at her best friend and next door neighbor of almost four years. Robyn was a few years younger than her own thirty-three and had long beautiful red hair and creamy white skin. While their backgrounds were different and there were at least five years between their ages, they had become pretty fast friends in a short period of time. "I have absolutely no idea."

"What about cooking? You love to cook."

"I guess."

"Well, in the meantime, stay with us," Robyn ordered.

"Oh Robyn, I can't do that to you and Erik."

"I already talked with Erik and he's fine with it. You can help me get the nursery ready for the new baby," Robyn told her, rubbing a hand over her stomach.

"I cannot impose on you…however, I will help you with the nursery," she grinned. "Remind me what Maddie's nursery looked like?"

Robyn described the decor of Maddie's room when she was born. It had recently been updated with new furniture and new paint.

"Hi ladies!" Erik Richards called as he came through the front door.

"Da!" Maddie shrieked and raced over to greet him.

"Hey there, Maddie-girl," he greeted her with a hug and a kiss on the cheek. He then turned to kiss his wife on the forehead. "Hi babe."

"Val refuses to move in with us," she told him without returning his greeting.

Valerie glared at her friend, "I am not going to impose on your family. Somehow I will find a solution to my problems."

"We should have just beat the crap out of that ex of yours. A man should take care of his wife, not steal from her." he grumbled. Sliding onto the couch next to Robyn, he petted the black lab that was begging for his attention. "When do you sell the house?"

"It goes on the market tomorrow," Val said sadly. "I'm going to miss that place." The house was only twelve years old and was on a nice half acre piece of property. It was the down-home family vibe that had drawn her to it initially.

"What are you going to do?" he asked as the phone rang.

Robyn grabbed the portable phone and answered it. "Hello?"

"I don't know, yet," she told him. Erik was as much her friend as Robyn, though she spent much more time with Robyn while Erik was at work. If she had picked out someone completely opposite in looks from Craig, it would have been Erik. They were both handsome, but Erik was dark-haired, dark-eyed and tan, while Craig had been a blond surfer-type.

"Okay." Robyn held out the phone to her husband. "It's your brother."

"Hi George." he said cheerfully, standing and leaving the room so as not to disturb the women's conversation.

"So, stay for dinner?" Robyn asked her friend.

"Only if I can help you make it," Val responded, catching Maddie in her arms. "What shall we have for dinner, Maddie?"

Maddie placed both her chubby little hands on either side of Val's face and said slowly. "Hot dogs."

Val laughed at her serious face. "I don't think Mommy and Daddy want hot dogs."

Maddie frowned and ran into the kitchen after her father. "Da! Hot dogs!"

Grinning, Robyn watched as her daughter attacked Erik's legs. "I think we have some chicken in the freezer."

"Stir fry?" Val suggested. "Do you have some fresh vegetables we can cut up?"

"Sure." Robyn stood and preceded Val into the kitchen. As they pulled food out of the refrigerator, Erik hung up the phone.

"Is everything all right?" Robyn asked as she put the frozen chicken breasts into the microwave to defrost.

He was staring at Val with an odd look on his face.

"Erik?"

16

Blinking, he turned his head to meet his wife's gaze. "What?"

"Is everything all right with George?" she repeated.

He leaned back against the counter, a smile spreading across his face. "Yeah. Old George is just in a little bind."

"What happened?"

Watching them flit around the kitchen, he paused to form his thoughts. "You remember Jennifer?"

"His nanny," she confirmed, scooping Maddie off the floor and setting her in her booster seat.

"Yeah, his nanny." He turned to look at Val's back as she stood at the sink washing vegetables. "She and her husband are moving to D.C.," he continued slowly.

Robyn turned back to him. He was looking at Val with a speculative gleam in his eyes. "Really? What is he going to do with Jessica?"

His eyes left Val and found his wife. "He needs to find a new nanny."

"Poor Jess...Jenny has been with them for two years," Robyn murmured.

"And she's such a sweet little girl," Erik responded. "So easy to care for."

Val froze. She could almost feel their eyes boring through the back of her skull.

"And he has such a nice big house in a friendly neighborhood." Erik strode across the room to take the plates out of his wife's hands to carry them to the table.

"Doesn't your brother live in Pennsylvania?" Val asked quietly.

"Yes, he does," Erik answered.

"You could start over, Val, someplace where no one knows your history," Robyn told her, not needing to remind her that the whole neighborhood knew about her very public marital and financial history.

"You want me to leave?" Val turned to her friend.

"No, I don't," she answered honestly. "But I do want what's best for you. It would be a good job in a good neighborhood...Jessica is a sweet little girl who would be lucky to have you."

"Well, Jenny is leaving at the end of the month," he told them as he set the table. "So you don't have to make any decisions right now."

"And I'm sure George would want to meet you before making any decision on his part," Robyn jumped in.

"Did you mention any of this to him?" Val asked, chopping carrots and celery at the same time.

"No, I didn't."

"So he might not even be interested in me."

Erik and Robyn exchanged smug looks behind Val's back.

"I don't really need a live-in," George said to his brother the next day.

Erik clutched the phone tighter. "She's a great person, George. She'd take good care of Jess."

"Does she have childcare experience?"

"She's taken care of Maddie hundreds of times," Erik responded.

"Why would she want to move to Pennsylvania for a job?" George wanted to know.

"She's had some financial trouble because of her ex-husband. She needs a job that offers her a place to stay."

Trouble with an ex George could understand. "I don't know..."

"Just meet her, George. What can it hurt to talk to the woman?"

"And she's okay with moving to Pennsylvania and living with strangers?"

Erik laughed. "I can't say she's thrilled...but she is interested in talking with you."

"Fine," George huffed. "Have her call me one evening after nine. Jess will be in bed and I can concentrate on talking to her."

"Great."

Chapter Two

Val wrung her hands together and stared at the phone. She was a naturally shy person so this call would be extra hard. The clock on the kitchen counter read nine-fifteen so she picked up the phone and dialed.

"Hello?"

Closing her eyes, she tried to picture an older version of Erik. "Yes, I'm looking for George Richards."

"This is he."

He sounded gruff and perturbed, like she had interrupted something important. "Hello, this is Val Adamson."

"Who?"

"Val...I'm a friend of your brother and sister-in-law," her voice was breathless with anxiety. Hadn't Erik said he'd spoken to George already?

"Oh, right," his tone softened. "Sorry. Somehow Erik and I never exchanged your name."

"Is this a good time to talk?"

"Sure," he paused. "Do you, uh, need me to call you back?"

Call her ba...oh damn, Erik had told him. "No, thank you," she said stiffly.

"I didn't mean to insult you," he said slowly. "I just thought it would be easier if I paid for the call."

He was just trying to be kind, she thought, *there was no need to be snippy with him.* "No, really, it's fine."

"All right."

When he was silent, she continued. "Why don't you tell me about your daughter."

"Jessica is four years old and just started preschool. She's very outgoing, loves to talk and color and play. Her favorite color is pink but she's definitely not a girlie-girl," he began.

"She likes to make mud-pies?" Val asked curiously.

He laughed. "Thank goodness, no. But she loves the jungle gym and the swings and isn't afraid to get dirty."

She shivered at the sound of his laugh. His voice was nothing like Erik's. "Too bad...I was a mud-pie girl and I loved every minute of it."

"I see. Well, like I said, Jess is in preschool now. That's three almost full days and two half days. I was expecting to be back in the office full-time this year but with Jennifer leaving, I'm reconsidering that plan."

"What kind of schedule do you keep now?" she asked curiously.

"I'm at work full days on Monday, Wednesday and Friday when Jess is in school until three. Tuesday and Thursday she's only at preschool until noon so I was working at home those two days," he answered.

"And what kind of schedule did you need from Jessica's nanny?"

"Well, Jennifer was picking up Jess on Mondays, Wednesdays and Fridays and staying with her until I got home. Sometimes she baby-sits other days when I need her. When I decided to go back to the office full-time, Jennifer offered to take over on Tuesdays and Thursdays also," he told her.

"So it's not *really* a live-in need," she said slowly.

"Well, I can certainly use extra help around the house if you were willing to do it," he suggested.

"Like what?"

"Light housekeeping like laundry, dishes and cooking duties."

Chewing on her lip, she wondered if this was really a good option. Move to Pennsylvania to keep house for a stranger? Was it a crazy idea? Was she crazy to even think about it?

"I wouldn't expect you to be a slave," he said suddenly. "Seriously, my first need is really someone to care for Jess."

"I don't want you to offer me this job because of something Erik told you about my situation," she said bluntly.

"I don't remember offering you a job, yet."

She smiled, liking his sense of humor. "Well, I'm still interested. When can I meet you and Jessica?"

"Why don't you come up for visit? We're only a few hours away," he offered.

She wondered if Robyn would let her borrow her car. Her own heap had already been sold. "Let me check on a few things and get back to you."

"Second thoughts?"

"No, I, uh, have to arrange for transportation," she mumbled.

"Okay. Let me know, then."

"It was nice speaking with you."

"Me, too, Valerie. Talk to you soon."

"Bye."

George hung up the phone and leaned back in his recliner. She seemed pleasant, if somewhat quiet. Could she handle Jess on a daily basis? Erik swore that she was good with Maddie, but Maddie was much younger. Well, he would meet her in person and see what his gut told him.

Val tucked her overnight bag into the small trunk of Robyn's sharp little convertible. The drive, she was told, was mostly highway and very easy. If she was comfortable, she would stay overnight at George's and come home Sunday. Home. She looked up at the house she still thought of as home. The sale sign in the front yard seemed huge and out of place. Sighing, she slid into the driver's seat and started the car.

George let Jessica help him make the bed in the guest room. In doing so, he knew it would take him twice as long to do the job, but she wanted to help and he wanted her to feel involved. Losing Jennifer was difficult enough, he didn't want to alienate Jess from what could be her new caregiver.

"Daddy?"

"Yes, sweets?"

"Can I put a chocolate candy on the pillow like when we stayed in that hotel?" she asked.

He grinned. She had talked about that chocolate candy for weeks. "Sure." When she scampered from the room, he stooped to straighten the comforter. It was a nice room, decorated to be neutral but comfortable.

Jessica ran back into the room, breathless from her trip down and then back up the stairs. "Here it is." Skipping to the head of the bed, she placed a wrapped chocolate on the pillow.

He smiled again. It was a full-size Crunch bar...her favorite. "That was very thoughtful of you, sweets."

"Thank you, Daddy," she said daintily.

"Would you like to play until Miss Adamson gets here?" he asked.

"All right." She skipped back out of the room and down the hall to her own bedroom.

"I'll call you when she gets here, okay?"

"'Kay."

He went downstairs, absently picking up a lone shoe to put away later. When the doorbell rang a minute later, he was still holding the small pink sneaker.

"Hello," Valerie greeted him when he threw open the door.

He stared at her for a moment, caught off guard. Blinking, he just stood there silently. She was older than he expected...not that she was *old* but he expected her to be in her early twenties. She was petite in comparison to his 6'4" frame, and very pretty in a girl-next-door kind of way. Her body was rounded in all the right places, filled out at the breasts and hips, screaming of womanhood. She had dark brown hair, sparkling green eyes and a warm complexion.

"Are you George Richards?" she asked tentatively as he continued to stare at her.

Shaking his head, he smiled, "Sorry, I wasn't expecting you for another hour or so." He stepped back and gestured for her to come in.

She looked at the shoe in his hand and grinned. "It's a little small, but a lovely shade of pink."

He was sure his jaw had dropped. When she smiled her whole face lit up. "Uh, oh." Laughing, he set the shoe aside and closed the door behind her. "How was the trip?"

"Great in Robyn's little ragtop."

"Good, good. Why don't you come sit in the family room," he suggested, leading her to the right.

Val followed him, noting his tall frame and long stride. He looked nothing like Erik that she could see...but he was handsome in his own right. His hair was short and brown, cut close in the back and parted on the right. When it got longer, she bet a cute lock would fall across his forehead. His eyes were hazel-colored and warm when he smiled. He fairly towered over her, making her feel almost small and feminine, even though her body was far from small. As she perched on the couch she looked around the room. It was neat and welcoming, decorated in greens, browns and tans. "You have a lovely house."

"Thank you," he responded from his seat on the recliner. They sat silently for a moment. "So, how long have you known Erik and Robyn?"

"About four years."

Nodding, he waited for her to elaborate. When she didn't, he frowned. "Are you a Maryland native?"

"Yup...born and bred."

"Do you still have family there?"

"Uh, no. My parents passed away when I was little."

"Only child?" When she nodded again, he stared at her. "Where did you grow up?"

"Foster homes," she said quietly.

"I'm sorry."

Smiling, she shook her head. "To tell you the truth, I didn't know anything else so it was no big deal. I had good foster families even though I moved around a bit."

"Okay." Pushing to his feet, he strode to the archway. "Jess! Come on downstairs, please." She didn't acknowledge him but a minute later they heard her come thumping down the stairs.

Screeching to a halt in the archway, she eyed the newcomer.

"Hello," she said politely.

"Hello, I'm Valerie Adamson."

"Valerie, this is my daughter, Jessica," he placed a big hand on her head. "Jess, this is Miss Adamson."

After getting a gentle shove, Jessica stepped forward to shake Val's hand. "Nice to meet you."

"It's very nice to meet *you*," Val responded. The little girl was adorable but looked nothing like her father. She was fine-boned with blond hair and wide blue eyes. "I like your socks."

Jess smiled and wriggled her toes inside her pink socks. "Thanks!"

"Were you playing upstairs?" Val asked, making eye contact with the bright little imp.

"Yup. Would you like to see my room?"

"You bet I would!" Val stood and took Jess' outstretched hand. They left the room and went upstairs toward the bedroom.

George wasn't surprised at his daughter's boldness. She was a happy, eager, outgoing child with a zest for life. In that way she was very much like the woman he had met and married before her birth. Unfortunately, motherhood had not agreed with Bernice and her whole attitude had changed. The divorce had been short and unemotional on both their parts. He was sad that Jessica would never know the vivacious woman he had met...but she would still have a wonderful life with him, he would make sure of that.

Val followed Jessica down the hall and into an amazingly pink room.

"This is my room," Jess announced.

"I bet I know what your favorite color is," Val grinned.

"Pink!"

"I see that." Pink walls, pink carpeting, pink curtains, pink bedding...her furniture was white with pink trim. "And who are these handsome people?" She pointed to a picture on the dresser.

"That's my Nana and Paw-Paw."

"And where do they live?"

"In a house," Jessica answered, plopping onto the floor.

24

Ah, the world of a child...everything in black and white, no shades of gray. She dropped to the floor across from Jessica. "What are you playing?"

She picked up a bear. "My daddy gave me this. It's my favorite."

"I like him...he looks very happy," Val responded.

"Do you have a bear?"

"I do have one or two at home," she nodded.

"Did your Daddy give it to you?"

"No. But I love it anyway."

"Where do you live?"

"Right next door to your Aunt Robyn and Uncle Erik."

Jess frowned, "They live far away. Jennifer is moving far away."

"I heard. But you know what?" Val whispered.

"What?" Jess leaned forward and whispered back.

"Just because she's moving far away doesn't mean she's far away from your heart. You won't love her any less and she most certainly won't love you any less."

George stood out in the hallway, listening to their conversation.

"But she won't be here anymore," Jess said sadly.

"No, she won't," Val answered simply. "And you'll miss her lots. It's okay to miss your friends when they go away. If I come here, I'll be leaving my friends, too. Maybe we can keep each other company and cheer each other up when we're sad."

"Really?"

"I'll tell you what. When you're missing Jennifer, you can tell me all about her and the fun things you did together. When I'm missing my friends, I'll tell you about them. Deal?" Val put out her hand.

"Deal," Jess grasped Val's hand and shook it hard.

"I thought I lost you two," George said from the doorway.

"Daddy, I'm hungry."

He looked at his watch, "I think it's a good time for ice cream."

Jessica jumped to her feet, "Yay!"

"Why don't you go find your shoes? I saw one in the family room," he called after her as she streaked from the room.

"Ice cream, huh?" Val said as she got to her feet.

She barely came up to his chin. "There's a DQ a few blocks from here. It's a nice day out and you can check out the neighborhood."

"All right." She followed him back downstairs. "You have a wonderful daughter."

"Thank you."

"What would be my responsibilities on the weekends?" she asked, trailing him into the family room.

"Daddy, I can't find my other shoe," Jess said from the floor.

"Did you look under the couch?" he suggested absently, his focus still on Valerie. "I'm happy to negotiate weekends with you. I'm usually home or at my parents' house so I can take care of Jess. But there might be times when I require your help. Pretty much it would be the same as evenings."

Val was thinking she might be able to get a second job somewhere. "You already know my car situation...how would we work that out?" she asked.

He grunted as he watched Jess scoot out from behind the couch with the missing pink shoe. How the hell had it ended up there? "Actually, I still have the car I bought for my ex-wife. It's a couple of years old, but it runs fine."

She caught her breath at the mention of his ex, but the casual tone of his voice never changed. "All right."

"I'm ready," Jess announced.

"Tie your shoe, Pinkie-Lee," Val directed.

"Who?" Jess asked, bending over to tie the offending lace.

"Pinkie-Lee...oh never mind," she grinned and took Jess' hand in hers. "It's ice cream time."

"Do you have a dog?"

George groaned at his daughter's question.

"Nope."

"I want a dog but Daddy says not yet."

They were out on the sidewalk, George following behind the two girls. "You're too young."

"You could pretend to have a dog. Each morning you can get up half an hour early, pretend to take it out back to do it's business, then pretend to bring it back inside and feed and water it," Val suggested.

"Get up early?" Jess wrinkled her nose.

"She's not a morning person," he whispered.

"Who is?"

He frowned, "I am."

"Hmph...give me a week and I'll show you the flaws of being a morning person," she told him. Looking around, she noticed that most of the houses were big but not ostentatious and had well-kept yards. Back at home, people did not linger in front of their houses, they just came home from work, parked their cars in their garages and went inside. Here she saw whole families outside, working in their yards, playing in the quiet street or talking with neighbors on the sidewalk. There was even a couple sitting on their porch, reading a book and the newspaper! How unfamiliar and yet comforting to see people living in today's society as a community rather than as individuals. Continuing farther, she saw that they were not the only ones on a mission for the local hangout. Families were either en-route or on a return trip from the Dairy Queen clutching dripping ice cream cones or milkshakes in Styrofoam cups. As they approached the DQ, she also saw that there were teenagers lounging near their bikes, eating ice cream and jostling each other as if they were straight out of the 50's. Could she live in a place like this?

"Daddy, I want vanilla."

"I want chocolate," Val joined in before standing off to the side with Jess' hand clutched in hers.

George groaned and walked up to the Dairy Queen window to order. When he returned he was juggling three cones. "Vanilla for the blond-haired lady...." He handed the sugar cone to his daughter. "Chocolate for the brown-haired lady...and mint chocolate chip for the gentleman."

They sat at one of the picnic tables in the parking lot.

"Do you do this often?" Val asked when she was done with her cone.

"Maybe once a month in the spring and summer. Not quite as often in the early fall when the weather is still nice," he answered.

"This is a nice neighborhood," she murmured. "Very quiet."

"We like it."

"How long have you been here?"

"I bought the house shortly before Jessica was born."

"Are your parents in the area?" she asked as they stood.

He wiped Jessica's face before they started back to the house. "They're about thirty minutes away."

"That's nice."

"Yes, I like having Jess' grandparents nearby." He swung Jess' hand in between their bodies. "You realize that I have to do a background check on you before I can offer you a job."

She frowned, "As long as you don't spread my personal problems around."

"Is there anything you want to tell me before I request the search?"

"My ex was a real jerk."

He nodded and fell silent.

"I'm a good person, George," she stated firmly. "But I won't let anyone walk all over me again."

"Are you still interested in the job?"

She smiled down at Jessica, then back up at him, "You bet."

Chapter
Three

Val did stay overnight but left just after breakfast Sunday morning. George promised he would call soon to confirm that he'd taken care of her background check. When a week had passed and there was no word, she was disappointed but not terribly surprised. She knew they really didn't need a full-time live-in nanny.

"I don't know what is wrong with George," Robyn told her over lunch the next week. "You'd be perfect for the job and he could really use the extra help."

Val shrugged and took a bite out of her cheese sandwich. "It's hard to work a stranger into your life full-time."

"He's nuts to pass you up. Look, our baby will be here soon...," Robyn began.

"Forget it."

"Seriously, Val, we could use your help. You can stay here with us and help out around here part-time."

Val shook her head, "I can't and won't do that to you guys."

"Val!"

In response, she turned to Maddie and grabbed her little hands, "Yes, honey?"

"Cheese!"

"Yes, I know. It's good cheese," Val answered with a grin.

"Have you had any bites on the house yet?"

Val nodded and absently wiped Maddie's cheek with her napkin. "We actually have two offers. Unfortunately, both are below asking price."

"By a lot?"

"Ten grand. The realtor thinks we should counter offer one of them and see what happens," she responded.

"Well, it can't hurt to try it, right?"

Nodding, Val watched Maddie stuff her cheese sandwich into her mouth. She sighed wistfully, half glad that she and Craig had never had kids...and half disappointed. She'd always wanted to have children.

"Hey," Robyn said suddenly. "Can you babysit for us Friday night? Erik has this thing for work..."

"Absolutely," Val answered. "I'm at your beck and call."

"Great. And maybe tomorrow you can come with me while I look for a new dress to fit my rapidly expanding waistline."

"Oh, you're beautiful and you know it!" Val exclaimed. "You were gorgeous carrying Maddie and you'll be fabulous while you're carrying this one."

"I look like an elephant when I'm pregnant...but at least I get to eat like a pig!" Robyn laughed.

"Pig! Oink!" Maddie crowed.

Val grinned and made snorting noises into Maddie's sweet-smelling neck.

"Maybe that's why George didn't hire you," Robyn teased her.

"Not attractive, huh?"

Shaking her head, Robyn eyed her friend. "And you...did you find him attractive?"

"He seemed nice," Val hedged.

"C'mon now...tell the truth. He's handsome, isn't he?"

"Sure. And he's good to his daughter...but I'm not in the market for a man," Valerie said firmly.

"Well, George does have his dark past," Robyn said, vaguely.

"Really? Do tell."

George pulled into the driveway and turned off the van. Checking his rear view mirror, he could see that Jess was completely asleep in her booster seat, her head slumped to the side. The ride hadn't been long, but she was always one to sleep in a moving vehicle.

Grunting, he unfolded himself from the car and closed the door softly. It took him only a few strides to reach the back passenger door and slide it open. "C'mon, sweets, time to go inside." He unbuckled her seatbelt and pulled her into his arms. Asleep, she was dead weight and he hiked her up and into a more comfortable position on his shoulder. Walking to the front door, he knocked. When no one answered, he knocked again, louder.

"Hold your horses," a female voice called.

He frowned. Erik knew he was coming, so what was the problem? When the door opened a crack, he peered inside. The eye that met his gaze was at once familiar yet unfamiliar. Robyn didn't have green eyes.

"George?" the voice asked uncertainly.

"Yeah," the eye blinked, then disappeared as they closed the door and unhooked the safety chain. When the door swung open again, he stood frozen on the front stoop. "Valerie?"

She smiled wryly and stepped back to let him in. "Hi."

"Am I at the wrong house?" he asked, stepping inside.

"No. Erik and Robyn are out and I'm babysitting Maddie," she answered

"Oh. I'm guessing by the look on your face they didn't tell you I was coming in for the weekend?" he muttered, striding into the family room and setting his daughter on the couch.

"Nope."

He covered Jess with a throw blanket then turned back to face her. "So, how are you?"

She crossed her arms in front of her chest, "I'm fine. You?"

Sighing, he perched on the arm of the couch, "A little tired, but otherwise we're fine."

"That's good." They were silent for a moment.

"I'm sorry I hadn't called you back, yet," he told her. "I never got a chance to run the background check."

"No problem, I understand. You really have no need for a full-time nanny, let alone a live-in," she said frostily.

"Actually, our current nanny got sick so I've been trying to work and take care of Jess all week," he sighed and closed his eyes. "If anything this past week has shown me how much help we do need. I never realized how much Jenny does for us during the week."

31

Her face softened and she relaxed a little. "I'm sorry that you had a bad week."

"Actually, we came down here to ask you to come live with us."

She blinked, "What?"

"We'd be thrilled to have you come live with us. Jess has been asking about you daily and I have to admit, you seem really great," he said.

"What about the background check?"

"I have two great references right here. And I would like to think that I'm a pretty good judge of character." He watched her face as he spoke, "You are still interested, aren't you?"

"Of course!" she exclaimed.

He heaved a sigh of relief, "Thank goodness."

"But there is one condition."

His gaze met hers. "Yes?"

"Don't say anything you don't mean."

One eyebrow went up. "Okay."

"I'm serious. If you don't mean something, don't say it. Be honest with me no matter what. I've had enough lies and broken promises in my life," she said vehemently.

"I promise that I will do my best," was his sincere response.

"Thank you."

"So, when can you start?" he asked eagerly.

She laughed. "I can be packed by Sunday."

"We can have your furniture shipped later," he offered.

"No need for that." She crossed the family room and went into the kitchen for some water.

"You don't want to bring anything with you?" he asked curiously, following behind her.

"Nothing to bring." She held out the water jug to offer him a drink.

Shaking his head, he leaned against the archway, "You sell everything?"

"Repossessed," she said curtly.

He was silent for a moment, "I'm sorry."

"Not your fault." Taking a long drink of water, she watched the emotions crossing his face. He was definitely curious, but way too polite to ask, she decided.

Shoving away from the wall, he turned away, "I'm going to put Jess to bed."

"Would you mind poking your head into Maddie's room? She's been sleeping for a couple of hours so she should be fine...but as long as you're up there..."

He nodded, "No problem." With that, he was gone.

She slid into the kitchen chair and stared at the empty archway. She got the job...she was leaving Maryland and moving in with two strangers. Was she doing the right thing? It was hard enough for two people who loved each other to live together...but two strangers?

George returned to the family room, so tired that he wanted to just lay down on the couch and sleep for a week. With a sigh, he looked into the kitchen to find Val sitting at the table there. "Hey."

She looked up. "Tucked in all right?"

Nodding, he sat down across from her, "You have anything you want to ask me?"

Grinning, she asked, "Do I have to wear a uniform?"

He laughed, "Nope."

"Do I have to do windows?"

"Not unless you want to."

"Am I expected to snake the drain?"

"I'm a pretty good home plumber, so no."

She tilted her head, "What *do* you do for a living?"

"Marketing," he answered vaguely.

"Do you travel a lot?"

"Nope."

"Chew with your mouth open?"

He grinned again, "My momma taught me better than that."

"Do you date a lot?"

His eyes flew to hers but there was only curiosity in her clear green gaze. "Not often."

"I was just wondering if I could get a second job for weekday evenings," she explained.

"You don't need a second job."

Frowning, she responded, "I'll make sure that Jess' care always comes first."

"You won't need a second job," he repeated firmly.

"I don't expect you to understand," she said softly. "But I need to have some money coming in to put away for my savings."

"You're coming to work for me and I'm going to pay you for that."

"Room and board was all I asked for," her voice was low.

"Live-in nannies get a salary as well."

"I am not going to take advantage of you or this situation," she said hotly.

He gazed at her, "This is not negotiable."

"Excuse me?"

"I mean it, Val. If you come to work for us, you work only for us. I can't have you distracted or overtired from a second job." He didn't raise his voice but there was no room for argument in his tone. "I'll pay you market rates for the job you'll be doing and expect you to honor my requirements."

She understood the theory behind his request but felt trapped by it. "George..."

"I meant what I said. This is not negotiable. We can work on time off, personal and sick days, even health insurance...but not this," he was adamant.

"All right," she relented. "But only because you asked so nicely."

He nodded and got to his feet, "I apologize, but I'm beat."

Waving him away, she remained in her chair, "I'll see you tomorrow."

"Good night, Val."

"Good night, George," she called softly.

"I'm really sorry," Erik told her later. "It just slipped my mind that he was driving down."

"It's fine...it was just a surprise."

"So," Robyn asked quietly. "What happened?"

"He asked me to come work for him."

Erik and his wife exchanged looks, "That's terrific!" he said.

"I'm going to miss you!" Robyn sniffled. "When are you leaving?"

"Sunday."

"Sunday!" Robyn and Erik echoed.

"No time like the present," she quipped.

"We'll all have to go out to dinner tomorrow night to say goodbye," Erik decided.

"I'll come over and help you pack tomorrow," Robyn offered.

"Not much left to pack," Val said wryly. "Most everything is already in boxes or suitcases."

"We'll tape up and mark the boxes for shipping or storage," she amended. "Oh, what am I going to do without you?!"

Erik patted her shoulder and smiled. "At least you still have me."

Robyn blinked once, then burst into tears.

Valerie hugged her friend and then stepped toward the front door. "Good night, you two."

"Good night, Val," Erik called as he led his hormone-ridden wife toward the stairs.

Val stepped out into the night air, thoughts swirling around in her head. She had spoken the truth, there was little left to pack at her house. But still, the thought of leaving was almost overwhelming. She was going to start a new life in a new state...where people knew nothing about her disastrous life with Craig.

Inside her house she walked through the empty foyer and upstairs to her bedroom. Once there she dropped to the mattress that was resting directly on the floor. She pried off her shoes and fell backward onto the bed. She had a job...a livelihood...a place to stay that had furniture. She was both excited and anxious at the thought of making such a huge change in her life. Beneath that, she was just a little nervous at having to live with George. Yes, she admitted, she found him attractive...he was handsome and intelligent and had a very gentle hand with his daughter. But she was *not* in the market for a man or a relationship. Besides all that, she was going to be working for him so a personal relationship was out of the question.

Closing her eyes, she rolled over onto her side and tried to empty her mind. As she drifted off to sleep, images of George danced through her mind.

George looked in his rear view mirror and caught sight of Val's dark head next to his daughter's blond one. She had chosen to ride in the back seat with Jess during the trip from Erik's house to his. Theirs. His.

"Let's try to think of food that starts with each letter of the alphabet," Val announced.

Jess frowned "Huh?"

"Like 'A' is for apple," Val said. "What kind of food starts with 'B'?"

Thinking for a moment, Jess' eyes brightened. "Banana!"

Val grinned, "Great! What comes next?"

"A, B, C!"

"What kind of food starts with a 'C'?"

When Jess didn't answer, George spoke up from the front seat, "What does Bugs Bunny eat?"

"Carrots."

"Good job, sweets!" he praised her.

They continued like that through most of the alphabet. When they hit "O", George and Val suddenly realized that Jessica had stopped contributing.

"Asleep," Val confirmed.

"She never could resist a moving automobile," George told her. "Why don't you climb up here and keep me company."

Val did so, stepping carefully between the two front seats to settle onto the passenger side.

"Speaking of automobiles...I've been thinking about our situation," he glanced over at her. "I think I'll just let you use the minivan. Jess' seat is already in here and it will be better to carry groceries and things. I'll drive the other car."

"Okay," Val responded simply.

"I didn't figure you'd be too keen on driving another woman's car, anyway."

She shrugged, "It's just a car."

"Well, it's really too small for your needs," he assured her.

"You bought her a sports car, huh?"

He flushed and kept his eyes on the road. "I guess you could call it that."

"Hmm, what is it? Maybe I *do* want to drive it," she grinned. "Is it a Beamer?"

Grunting, he checked his mirror before changing lanes, "No, but it is a convertible."

"Ooo...remember how we talked about negotiable items?" she said teasingly.

"We'll talk about it later."

She looked out the side window for a moment before speaking again. "May I ask you a question?"

"Shoot."

"What happened to Jessica's mother?"

He frowned and looked at his daughter in his rear view mirror, "Bernice is no longer a part of our lives."

"Her choice or yours?"

"Bernice was young when we met...she got pregnant almost right away. I did what I thought was right and married her," he said bluntly. "She seemed happy enough. I told her she could have whatever she wanted...stay home with the baby, go back to school, work, whatever. I bought the house right after we were married, and then the car soon after that. Things seemed fine until after Jess was born. I was thrilled," he said softly. "Bernice just seemed uninterested. I thought she would warm up, but she didn't. I offered her whatever she wanted...," he trailed off.

"What did she want?" Val whispered.

"She wanted to be free."

Val looked at the little girl in the backseat and frowned.

"So we drew up the divorce papers and she signed away all rights to Jess. The next day, she was gone."

"No word since then?"

"Nope."

"What will you tell Jessica about her mother?" she asked curiously.

"That her mother loved her and was a beautiful person, but that she was too young to raise a child," he responded.

"I'm sorry."

Shaking his head, he continued, "I'm not. I think I'm giving my daughter a good life, filled with love and support. I can't be sorry for what happened...it brought me Jess."

"I think you're doing a terrific job with Jessica," she said sincerely.

"Thank you." After a few minutes of silence, he spoke again, "May I ask *you* a question?"

"Sure."

"What happened with you and your ex-husband?"

Chapter
Four

Her eyes flew to his face, "Well, I'm surprised."

"At what?"

"I thought you were too polite to ask."

He just shrugged and remained silent.

"I was always plump and used to be a very quiet and shy person...more so than I am now. I was living in a tiny apartment, working a low-paying job and just surviving," she began. "I was twenty-six when I met Craig. He was loud and flamboyant and spontaneous. I never expected a man like him to pay attention to someone like me, but he took me out to fun places and showed me a life I never knew existed. I was overwhelmed by him...I thought I loved him. We eloped soon after and he moved into my apartment." She saw his face and sighed, "Craig had a job, trust me. He knew my background and my livelihood...he didn't marry me for money."

"What did he do for a living?"

"He was in sales. After a few years we moved into a bigger place. I was happy because Craig was fun and we were really living. He wanted a house so we weren't in the bigger apartment for very long. Since I wasn't good with money, he took over our finances." She laughed wryly when she heard George groan. "He promised to take care of everything. We bought the house and he helped me pick out furniture and decorations...all on credit cards. For a while I ignored the doubts...he was in sales and you could make a lot of money in sales. But when he bought the big car, I started getting nervous. I knew he wanted to impress the clients he saw with his car...could I blame him?"

"What happened after that?"

"They came to the front door about two months later. They wanted to know where the car was. I told them the truth...Craig had it at work," she sighed. "They sat out front and waited for him. When he got home, they loaded up the car and took it away. All the while, Craig is screaming bloody murder. He swore to me that it was a mistake and that he would get it all straightened out. It turns out the mistake was that Craig had bounced the deposit check and hadn't made one payment. The next week, they came for the furniture and I called him at work as they were carrying things out. He came home, in my car, and walked through the front door. He stood in our kitchen and told me he couldn't live like this anymore. He packed a bag, called a taxi and left."

"What?" his voice was low and harsh. "He just left you to deal with the collection agencies?"

"And more. I found out he had two mortgages on the house and credit card debt out the wazoo. I went to a women's assistance facility and got a lawyer. She tracked Craig down and served him the divorce papers. Fortunately for me, most of the credit cards were in his name only. But the house and the car...well, lets just say my credit stinks now."

"Did he clean out your bank accounts?"

She laughed, "What bank accounts? Everything was on credit. I sold my car so I could have a little cash."

"The house?"

"I'm hoping the sale will just pay off the two mortgages," she told him honestly.

"Whew, he really did a number on you."

"Yeah," she said softly. "And I still don't know why. I thought he loved me."

"Did you really love him?"

"I thought so. After he left, I wondered if it was his flamboyant, spontaneous nature that I loved."

"And?"

"I'm still not sure."

He nodded and they fell silent. "Val?" he called her name sometime later.

"Yeah?"

"Not all men are like your ex."

She nodded, "I know that."

"Good."

Val stood in her new beige bedroom, her suitcases lined up neatly in front of the closet. The remainder of the car ride had been uneventful. Upon arriving home, George had first carried Jessica upstairs to her bedroom, then returned to carry Val's suitcases inside. After setting the last bag down in her room, he left her to get settled.

The room was nice, unassuming and very neat. The queen size bed was dressed in a sage green comforter that neither looked new nor old and there was a matching filmy green sheer hanging down over the window. She could make a few changes and easily claim the room as her own, but she wasn't sure she was ready to do that. Instead she quietly unpacked her clothes into the one closet and dresser, tucking away her emptied suitcases under the bed. When she was done, she sat down on the side of the mattress and heaved a sigh. Nothing would never be the same.

She looked up when she heard a noise coming from the doorway. There Jessica stood, thumb in her mouth, sleep-softened eyes focused on Val's face. "Hi, sweetie."

Jess sniffled and spoke around her thumb, "You look sad," she lisped.

Val smiled and beckoned her forward, "I am a little sad, honey." She pulled Jess into her arms. "I've left my friends and my old house to come live with you."

"Do you want to talk about them?" she asked, eyes wide with concern.

Hugging the small form closer, she was amazed that Jess remembered their conversation. "Maybe another time, okay?"

"'Kay." She stepped out of Val's arms. "I'm thirsty."

Val grinned at the announcement and stood, "Then lets go find a drink."

They clattered down the stairs together and into the kitchen. As she searched the cabinets for juice glasses, she took a few minutes to look around the room. Like many of the other rooms in the house, she noticed that this room was bright and clean, if a bit cluttered. The cabinets were a plain oak and the ones above the beige counter were quite tall with lots of storage, some of which was empty. She couldn't imagine having empty cabinets as every one in her home with Craig has been filled to capacity, and then some! But as she found out, George was not in the habit of entertaining...he had enough items to comfortably care for himself and for Jessica, but that was it.

Val was still puttering around when George walked in.

"Hi."

"Hi, Daddy. Valerie gots me a drink."

"That's very nice of her," he answered his daughter. "You finding everything okay?"

"Yup...no problem. You want a drink, too, Dad?" she teased.

"Uh, no, thanks." He turned back to his daughter, "What would you like for dinner?"

"Hot dogs!" was her pat answer.

He groaned, "How about something else?"

She gave it some thought, "Pizza."

"I can make something," Val offered.

"Not tonight. You should get settled in before having to think about that stuff. Besides," he said sheepishly. "You'll need to go grocery shopping tomorrow."

"Pizza," Jess repeated, finishing her juice.

"And what would you like on your pizza, little bit?" he asked.

"Cheese," she answered matter-of-factly.

Val laughed out loud, "At least she says what she means."

He grinned, "How about pepperoni?"

"'Kay."

"Val?"

"Fine with me," she answered. "Do you mind if I just scout around while we're waiting for it to arrive?"

"Mi casa es su casa."

"Daddy," Jess tugged on his shirt. "What does that mean?"

As he was explaining, Val wandered into the pantry to see what he had stored in there. Her next foray was through the kitchen cabinets beneath the plain counter tops. She tried to familiarize herself with his setup and his tools. His kitchen was well stocked with pots and pans but lacked the 'fun' accessories. "You don't have a mixer or a blender."

He frowned, "For what?"

"No bread machine or ice cream maker," she continued her list. "No crockpot or pasta maker."

"I have a waffle maker," he defended himself.

"Yes, I saw your Mickey Mouse waffle iron," she told him. "It's very nice."

"We're not fancy people here."

"I can have Robyn send up some of my kitchen equipment next week. There's nothing like the smell of fresh-baked bread," she said, making a mental note to call her best friend that night.

"You can buy whatever we need," he corrected her. "I'll give you my charge card."

"No need. I'm quite comfortable with my own equipment."

He shrugged and went back to reading the paper. "By the way, I'll get you a credit card to go grocery shopping and for anything else you buy for the household."

"I'm going to need a budget," she requested.

"Don't worry about it," he said absently.

"I'm serious, George. I'm going to need a monthly budget for things I'm responsible for. I'm also going to need to know if you or Jess are allergic to anything."

Looking up, he caught the expression on her face, "All right, we'll work out a food budget."

She nodded and went back to inspecting the kitchen. The refrigerator was almost empty and needed a good cleaning. "Are the washer and dryer in the basement?" she asked him.

"No, they're over there," he indicated a door that led into a small square laundry room.

"And when do you get moving in the morning?"

"I'm usually up by six but Jess doesn't get up until seven fifteen. Preschool starts at eight thirty." Turning the page, he continued, "I'll go in with you two tomorrow morning to let the staff know they can release Jess to you each day."

"All right. And what do you two eat for breakfast?" she wanted to know.

"Jess will eat pretty much anything, including cold cereal. I usually just have coffee."

She tsked, but made no comment. "What time do you eat dinner?"

"We're pretty flexible." He set down the paper and turned to look at her, "You can relax, Val, we're not tyrants."

"I want to have as little disruption in your lives as possible. I'm here to help, not hinder," she said flatly.

"It'll be fine, don't worry." When the doorbell rang, he went to answer it.

Val followed him with her eyes until he disappeared from view. With a deep sigh, she turned to set the table in the breakfast nook for dinner.

It was dark and quiet in the house as Val rolled over in bed. Her alarm clock read five forty-five a.m. She would wait until she heard George moving around before getting up. As was her normal habit, she had showered the night before to save time in the mornings. When she heard the shower turn on about thirty minutes later, she slipped out of bed. Dressing in the semi-darkness, she carried her brush down the hall to the bathroom she shared with Jessica. It took her only a few minutes to wash her face, brush her teeth and hair, then wipe down the bathroom sink. She was downstairs in the kitchen before the shower in the master bedroom shut off. Starting a pot of coffee, she went about making toast and getting Jess' cereal ready.

George came striding into the kitchen and froze. "Good morning," he said finally.

"Good morning," she responded. "Coffee should be ready shortly."

"You don't have to make me coffee."

"I drink it too, you know," she told him wryly.

He flushed and crossed to pull two cups out of the cabinet. "I'm not accustomed to having another adult in the house," he apologized.

"No problem."

"You need cream or sugar?" he offered.

"No, I need a clean shot of caffeine in the morning," She yawned, then grinned.

"What are your plans for the day?" he handed her a full cup of black coffee.

"I should go to the grocery store...you have no food here."

He smiled and took a gulp of his hot coffee. "I'll give you my credit card to take care of food today."

"Anything special you like to eat?"

"Jess likes frosted flakes for breakfast. And she eats Fruit Loops as a snack. Otherwise we're pretty simple folk."

"Whole milk?"

"Yep."

"Eggs, muffins?"

"Sure. Honestly, we eat pretty much everything," he assured her.

"Okay, okay!" She held up her hand, "I got it. I'm going to wake Jessica."

"Be aware that she's slow to come to," he warned.

"All right, thanks."

He watched her leave, thinking how nice it was to come downstairs to an adult conversation. And to tell the truth, she was easy on the eyes. While she was short in stature, she had a solid strength about her that he admired. What was it going to be like living with her on a day-to-day basis? So far, she seemed conscientious and good-humored...and she was definitely going to need both those attributes for this job.

Val dropped Jess off at preschool and made her trip to the grocery store. She bought as much fresh food as possible, then added some sorbet and ice cream to her cart. When she was at home unpacking, she began making a list of meals that she could prepare. She loved to cook and was happy to have a new and open audience.

Standing in the silent kitchen, she sliced peaches for the waiting piecrust. She could get used to this, she thought, cooking and caring

45

for the family that belonged to her. With a frown she laid out the peaches in the piecrust and added flour and sugar. She covered the pie with what she hoped would turn out to be a nice flaky dough and pinched the sides together. Brushing the top with a quick eggwash, she set the oven and put the pie inside. She would make the fresh whipped cream later to go with the french vanilla ice cream she'd bought.

With that completed, she left some chicken breasts to marinate and went upstairs. She had left her bed undone this morning so now she took the time to make it. Peeking into Jess' room, she straightened her bedclothes as well. A quick stop in the bathroom and then she was done. Striding past George's room, she saw that his bed was unmade as well. Without giving it further consideration, she walked in and made his bed. Touching his sheets almost felt like she was intruding on his privacy, but she shook the thought away. She would be doing his laundry...washing his underwear...she had to make these chores impersonal. Once the bed was made, she lingered for a moment to look around. His room was fairly neat and devoid of any decorations, but it was definitely male. If she inhaled deeply enough, she could smell him. Groaning, she scurried from the room.

George walked through the front door and immediately his mouth began to water.

"Daddy!" Jessica came flying out from the kitchen to greet him.

"Hi, sweets!" he gave her a kiss, then straightened.

"We're making dinner," she announced gaily.

"It smells wonderful, babe," he followed her into the kitchen. "Hi."

Val turned and smiled at him, "Hi there."

"Something smells delicious," he told her.

"Well, we hope you're hungry!"

He nodded, "You bet. Do I have time to change clothes?"

"Yup."

He hurried upstairs and changed from his suit into jeans and tee shirt then padded back downstairs barefoot. "Can I help with anything?"

"Everything is done," Val answered. "I had a great helper." She smiled down at Jess.

"Wait until you see the biscuits we made, Daddy," Jess said as she climbed up onto her chair.

"You made biscuits?" he was almost drooling. "From one of those cans?"

"Can?" Val made a face. "No way. Jessica and I made *real* biscuits."

He was sure he was drooling now. "No," he whispered reverently.

"Yup." She brought a dish of fresh steamed string beans that she and Jess had snapped together. Next she brought out the baked chicken that she had marinated earlier. The last thing she brought to the table was a basket of biscuits. "Ready to eat?"

"Oh yeah," he breathed, sliding onto his chair. He pulled a warm biscuit from the basket and brought it to his nose. "Yum."

"See the shape, Daddy?" Jess crowed. "I did that!"

Studying the biscuit, he realized it was the shape of a flower. "It's beautiful, sweets." What a great idea it was to involve Jess in making dinner. He broke open the light bread and inhaled the fragrant steam that came out of it. "What is that delicious smell?"

"Chives," Val answered. "Taste it."

He took a bite and groaned. It was light and buttery with just a hint of chive and it melted on his tongue. "Oh my."

"I want a star," Jessica requested.

Val found one for her, then took a plain round one for herself. Next she doled out her baked chicken and added the string beans.

"Everything is fabulous, Val. Thank you for a wonderful dinner," he praised her, shoveling food into his mouth.

"And thank you, Jessica, for all your assistance in the kitchen this afternoon," Val responded.

"Welcome," Jessica sang, mouth full of food.

As they were cleaning up after dinner, George spotted the pie. "Oh, no."

"What?"

He groaned. "What is that?"

"Pie."

"Why didn't you warn me? I'm so stuffed from dinner," he complained.

"It can wait until later," she assured him.

"If it's half as good as dinner, I'm going to be ill tomorrow."

"George?"

"Yeah?"

"What did you guys *used* to eat?" she asked delicately.

"Macaroni and cheese from a box," he answered. "Hot dogs, hamburgers, fish sticks...that kind of stuff."

"I see."

"Don't get me wrong, that stuff is fine...but what you did tonight was incredible."

"You don't like to cook?"

He frowned, "I never really had time. I would just make something quick and easy."

"Well, I enjoy cooking. So get used to it," she ordered.

"Yes, ma'am. And by the way," he said as he was leaving the kitchen. "Thanks for making my bed."

She flushed and ducked her head,"No problem."

"You don't have to. I'm not a stickler for made beds," he called.

"I'll remember that," she responded, wiping down the counter top with a paper towel.

He wandered into the family room where Jess was watching TV. When he went upstairs to change clothes before dinner, he'd noticed right away that she had been in his room. Besides the fact that his bed was neatly made, he could almost sense her presence. He wondered if she had looked around...if she had touched anything. Sinking into his recliner, he listened to her puttering around in the kitchen. It was almost comforting to have Valerie around. He felt like he finally had help in his life...someone to share in the responsibilities of caring for and raising his child.

Whew, he thought, he had better be careful what he was thinking. He could easily be taken in by this surreal family that they had created.

Chapter
Five

The weekday pattern was easy to establish. Val worked around the house, cooked, spent time with Jess, then had dinner. After dinner she made herself scarce, allowing George to spend time alone with his daughter. While Val was happy to turn down the beds and clean up after bath-time, she left George to perform the actual duties of bath and tuck-in. She knew those times were precious to both father and daughter and was loathe to interrupt.

Friday afternoon, some packages arrived from Robyn. They included her bread machine and her mixer. The note that came along indicated that they had yet to find the other requested items.

It didn't matter, Val was thrilled with these two appliances. She immediately unpacked them, then inspected them carefully to make sure they survived the trip in tact. She only tore herself away to go pick up Jess from preschool and stop at the grocery store for supplies.

Back in the kitchen, Val instructed Jess to wash her hands.

"What are we making?" Jessica asked, climbing onto her step stool at the kitchen sink.

"I think we should start with cookies. What do you think?" Val asked, setting up her mixer on the counter.

"What kind of cookies?"

Val grinned at the excitement in her voice, "Hmm, chocolate chip?"

"Yum!" Jess said happily, skipping over to the table where Val was setting up ingredients and bowls. "Can we have cookies for dinner?"

Laughing, Val started measuring dry ingredients and handing them to Jess. "Pour that into the big bowl."

Jess knelt on the chair and dumped flour into the big bowl. "Daddy loves chocolate chip cookies."

"Not for dinner, babe."

"No, really, he *loves* them," Jess insisted.

"I'm sure he does," Val responded easily. "But chocolate chip cookies are for dessert, okay?"

She sniffed unhappily but continued to help making the cookies.

Once the dough was finished, Val showed Jess how to scoop out the cookies from the bowl and onto the cookie sheet.

"These don't look like cookies," Jess complained.

"They will, don't worry."

Frowning, Jess put another lump of dough on the pan. "When?"

"In the oven. I'll show you once we put the cookies inside," Val reassured her.

"When can I eat one?" Jess wanted to know.

"Soon," Val promised, picking up the filled cookie sheet and sliding it into the oven. She grabbed a kitchen chair and scooted it across the room to the oven. "Come watch."

Jess climbed up onto the chair and peered through the glass door into the lighted oven. She sucked in a lip as the cookies melted and flattened. "Oh! Cookies! How did that happen?"

"It's magic!" Val told her, watching the cookies as well. "They smell good, don't they?"

"They smell incredible."

Val whirled around to see George standing just inside the kitchen.

"Daddy!" Jess jumped off the chair and flew into his arms.

"Y...you're early," Val stammered.

"I thought I would come home and take my lovely ladies out for dinner and a movie," he said, hugging Jess in his arms. He buried his nose in her hair and inhaled. "You, my darling, smell like cookies."

She giggled and wrapped her arms around his neck. "Chocolate chip cookies."

Groaning, he muttered, "My favorite."

Val checked the cookies, then stepped away to prepare the next sheet. "It's a good thing because we made plenty."

"So how about it?" he asked, setting Jess back onto the floor.

"How about what?"

"Dinner, movie..."

"Oh...well..."

"C'mon, you deserve a break," he prodded her.

She quickly exchanged cookie sheets, then shut the oven. "Why don't you two go have a fun night out?"

He frowned, "Why would we go without you?"

"Please come," Jess begged.

Val stood over the hot pan, chewing on her lip. There was really no reason for her to go...she wasn't part of the family. She was the hired help and needed to remember her boundaries. But then, they were her only friends in Pennsylvania. If she didn't go out and have fun with them, who would she go out with? She stalled a little longer, scraping the cookies off the pan and sliding them onto cooling racks.

"Val..."

Looking up, she met his gaze, "All right."

"Yay!" Jess clapped her hands. "Can we go to McDonalds?"

George laughed. "Maybe we can think of a little nicer place than that."

Putting more cookie blobs onto the now empty cookie sheet, Val smiled. "There's someplace nicer than Mickey D's?"

"I'm sure we can think of something," he teased, slipping around her and stealing a warm cookie from the cooling rack.

She smacked at his hand, then softened when he broke the cookie in half and gave the other half to his daughter. He was so good with her!

"Mmm," he moaned, the cookie practically melting in his mouth. "Tell me why you aren't a chef."

"They wouldn't let me sleep in the restaurant," she answered in a falsely disgusted voice.

"Mmm...their loss," he snitched another cookie before leaving to change his clothes.

She watched him go, then turned back to finish dealing with her cookies.

Taking one last look at herself in the mirror, Val left her room and tripped lightly down the stairs. She found George and Jess waiting for her in the family room.

George looked up at her arrival. "Hey."

"I'm ready."

He thought he nodded, but he wasn't sure. She was wearing a dark blue skirt that just covered her knees but made her legs look long and smooth. It hugged her generous hips and thighs without a wrinkle. On top she was wearing a light blue vee necked sweater with short sleeves. It revealed a lovely view of cleavage and dipped nicely at her waist before coming to rest at her hips. Her brown hair was loose and hung down just past her shoulders. When she smiled at him, her eyes lit up.

"Are we going?" she asked again.

"Daddy," Jess tugged at his hand. "Lets go."

He shook his head and got to his feet. "Yes, yes, we're going." Digging in his suddenly too tight jeans, he pulled his keys out of his pocket, "I found a nice place to eat dinner before the movie. It's an American restaurant that has hamburgers and chicken and fish. And we don't have to order dinner at a counter."

"Sounds like a plan. Have we picked a movie?" Val wanted to know as they walked outside to the minivan.

"I want to see the new Disney movie," Jess piped up.

"I love Disney movies," Val exclaimed.

George shot her a look of horror as he unlocked the car door.

"Really, I do!"

He groaned and rolled his eyes as he helped Jess into her seat. "I guess I'm out-voted."

Val smiled then climbed into the front seat. She was just getting ready to pull the door closed when George stepped up next to her. Her eyes found his, then widened in surprise.

"You look really great," he said softly, his eyes focused only on her face.

Blushing, she smoothed her hands over her skirt. "Thank you."

He stood there for a moment before backing away and closing her door.

Val watched him walk around the front of the van. She wasn't wearing anything unusual, though she had taken to wearing more casual clothes recently. Running around with Jess and cleaning house didn't exactly require her to wear a skirt and heels. She looked over at him when he slid in behind the steering wheel. Under other circumstances she could really like him, but he was her boss and she owed him her livelihood.

George carried his daughter through the front door and turned to see if Valerie was following. She strode in behind him, then closed and locked the door. When she turned back toward him, he was still standing there, watching her.

"Thank you for a lovely evening," she whispered.

"Thank you for coming with us. We both enjoy your company," he whispered back.

"Do you need help getting her into her pajamas?"

He shook his head, "She's pretty flexible."

Smiling, she twisted her hands together and took a step to the left. "Well, good night then."

"Coffee," he said suddenly. "I could really do with a cup of coffee."

"Coffee?" she repeated dumbly.

"And maybe some cookies?" his voice was hopeful and there was a teasing glint in his eyes.

"Sure. I'll, uh, put up a pot of coffee."

He started toward the stairs. "Decaf," he called over his shoulder.

She nodded at his back and walked into the kitchen. Pausing just inside the room, she slipped off her sandals. Ah, that was better. It took her just a few minutes to put up some coffee and place a handful of cookies on a plate. She was sitting at the kitchen table in the dark when George joined her.

"You want milk with your coffee?" he asked, standing next to the pot of freshly brewed coffee.

"Sugar too, please."

He brought her a mug of coffee along with the milk and sugar. "I forgot to tell you that we usually have dinner at my parents' house on

Sundays."

"That must be wonderful for Jess, that you're so close," she murmured, grabbing a cookie and breaking it in half.

"My parents love it, too," he paused to stuff a whole cookie into his mouth. "So we usually leave here around five."

"I'll make sure Jess is ready," she offered.

"No, I can get Jess ready."

"Oh, okay. I'll expect to have the house to myself for a few hours, then."

His cup was halfway to his mouth when he halted. Looking at her fiddling with half a cookie, he wondered where he had lost her. With a thunk, his cup hit the table. "I was telling you so *you* would be ready by five."

"Oh, no!" she exclaimed, dropping the cookie onto her napkin. "I couldn't impose."

"You're coming with us," he said firmly.

She was already shaking her head. "Thank you, but no. I have plenty of things to do Sunday."

He frowned but did not comment.

With a small sigh, she stood and placed her coffee cup in the sink. "I'll clean up in the morning," she said. "Thank you again for this evening. Good night."

He nodded but did not say anything else. When she was gone, he stood and cleaned up the kitchen. Why didn't she want to go with them? He thought they were getting along great and his parents were interested in meeting Jessica's new caregiver. He wasn't requiring that she spend the weekend watching Jess or cleaning the house...couldn't she spare a few hours to meet his family?

He was slow in climbing the stairs to his bedroom. As he was walking toward the room, he saw that Val's light was on. He wanted to stalk down the hall and demand an answer from her...but instead he entered his room. Softly, he closed the door then sank down onto his bed. It was neatly made again even though he had left it a shambles this morning. His sleep this past week had been restless with dreams but he refused to acknowledge the fact that those dreams were filled with erotic images of his daughter's nanny. However, considering the way she looked this evening, he wouldn't be surprised to see her face again tonight.

When Jess and George went out on Saturday, Val made a cake for them to take to dinner on Sunday. While the cake was baking, she went about making frosting. Cooking was a soothing task for her. Her favorite foster homes were the ones where one or both of the parents cooked. The best ones were the ones where she was allowed to be involved. That was exactly the reason that she frequently involved Jess in her cooking escapades. It didn't matter what it was, the power of creation was what moved her and she was entirely in control in the kitchen. Her ex could say a lot of things about their marriage, but he could never say he went hungry.

The timer went off and she scrambled over to take the three cake pans from the oven. Setting them aside to cool, she returned to the frosting. In the back of her mind, she was already planning the dinner menu for that evening. She had a nice piece of fresh fish in the fridge that she could bake.

She tested the frosting, then set it aside to check the cakes. They would require a little more time to cool so she set off upstairs to make the beds. It wasn't the first thing she did every day, but she did make it a point to straighten the beds each day. As usual, she left George's room for last. His sheets were extremely tangled and his comforter was half on the floor. With a tsking noise, she bent over to straighten the sheet first. Tugging it toward the top of the bed, she froze. She could smell him every time she neared the bed. It was a warm male smell that made her nose twitch. Hurriedly she snapped the sheet taught, then reached for the comforter. It was soft under her hands and she had a terrible urge to curl up underneath it. Instead she smoothed out the material then left the room. She had yet to enter his bathroom to clean it, and he had yet to ask her to. It seemed more personal than his sparse bedroom so she had avoided it all week.

Back downstairs she started frosting the first cake layer. She was pleased with how the cake had turned out. She wanted to make it perfect for George to take to his parents' house.

She was just finishing the final application of frosting when she heard the front door. Footsteps along the hall announced Jess' appearance.

"Val!"

"Jess!" she returned with a smile.

"Daddy and I went shopping."

George appeared a minute later. "And we know how much Daddy loves to shop."

"What did you buy?" Val asked, covering her cake in her plastic cake container.

"I got new socks," she said happily, pulling a package of colorful socks from her bag. "And Daddy bought new underwears."

He blushed and rolled his eyes, "Big mouth."

"I bet your socks are prettier than Daddy's underwear," Val teased.

"I wanted new shoes," Jess continued, unaware that her father's face was beet red. "But we couldn't find any."

"You couldn't find *any* shoes anywhere?" Val injected a note of incredulity into her voice.

"We found lots of shoes! But none that I liked," Jess explained.

"Oh, I see. Well, I can take you out again next week to look some more," Val suggested.

"Bless you," George muttered under his breath.

"It's no problem." She put the last of her utensils in the sink.

"What did you make?" Jess eyed the green cake container with undisguised glee.

"That's for you to take to your Nana and Paw-Paw tomorrow."

George's eyebrows shot up, "What?"

"I made a cake for you guys to take to dinner tomorrow night," she repeated, wiping down the counter tops.

"But you won't take it over yourself?" he questioned.

"Why would I?"

He frowned at her, "Why would you make a cake for strangers?"

"They're your parents."

"So why won't you come to dinner with us?" he wanted to know.

"That's family."

"You're a part of our family."

She shook her head, "No, I'm not. And that's okay, George."

He was about to respond when he noticed Jess watching them intently. "Sweets, why don't you go upstairs and put your new socks in your dresser," he suggested.

"Don't you like Nana and Paw-Paw?" the child wanted to know.

"Honey, I don't even know them," Val said softly.

"You should know them," Jess said simply before skipping out of the room with her package of socks.

"I could not have said it better myself," he muttered before leaving the room.

Val stood at the kitchen sink wondering when she had become the bad person in the house.

Chapter
Six

Val was stripping her bed the next day when George came to a halt in her doorway.

"We're leaving," he announced flatly.

She looked up, a lock of hair falling across her forehead. Wow, he looked good. He was wearing a pair of khakis and a brown polo shirt. His hair was neatly combed and his face was freshly shaved. She wanted to run over to him and bury her face in his neck...she was sure it would smell delicious. Swallowing tightly, she nodded. "Don't forget the cake."

"Right." He stood silently for a moment, staring at her. "We'll be back in a couple of hours."

"Have a nice time," she offered, straightening with her sheets bundled in her arms.

He gave her a curt nod and left.

Val sighed softly and stuffed her sheets into her laundry basket. Carrying it into the hallway, she dropped it onto the floor and entered Jess' room. Stripping her small bed was easy and she added the sheets to her own laundry basket. She had washed both her clothes and Jessica's yesterday so all she had now was bedclothes. Chewing on her lip, she stared down the hall at the door to George's room. It took her several strides to reach the door and a few more to his bedside. She bent slightly and began pulling the sheets off his bed. As she did so, she looked around the room for his clothes hamper. She hadn't done his laundry yet and he hadn't asked her to. After a quick search of his room and closet, she still hadn't found the hamper. Across the room the door to George's bathroom stood open. She hadn't been inside his bathroom yet, but now she had no choice. If she expected to do his laundry, she had to go in.

She stepped into the bright room and her mouth fell open. In comparison to his fairly plain bedroom, his bathroom was amazing. It was huge with a beautiful white corner tub, a bronze and glass shower stall and a marble counter top with two sinks. The tile on the floor was a veined gray and white marble and sparkled under the bright lights. There was no question, he kept the space neat and clean, with the towels folded primly in place. Grunting, she spotted the clothes hamper across the room. On the way she grabbed the towels and threw them on top of the hamper. Clutching the container, she left the room. It took her two trips to carry all the dirty laundry downstairs to the washer.

She had to get past this, she thought as she stuffed sheets into the washing machine. She really had no need for a man in her life. She needed to take charge and care for herself...find her own joy and excitement.

Shuffling back into the kitchen, she opened the refrigerator and peered inside. It was much easier to plan and make dinner when there were people to eat it. She pulled out a container of yogurt and grabbed a banana. This would do for the time being.

George tucked his daughter into her bed, then straightened. As usual, dinner at his parents' house had been pleasant, although this week they had peppered him with questions about Valerie. Her cake had been a hit for dessert and his father had begged him to leave the leftovers.

Incredibly, his mother had understood Val's reluctance to join them for dinner. But even after discussing it thoroughly, George still couldn't grasp the reasoning.

With a tired sigh, he crossed the hall and entered his bedroom. He clicked the light on and stopped short. His bed was neatly made and turned down on the side closest to the bathroom door. In addition, there were neatly folded stacks of clean clothes and towels lined up on the end of the bed. He stepped up to the bed and picked up the first stack and put it away. Did this mean she had washed his sheets as well? They had never really discussed what housekeeping duties she would perform...she just seemed to do whatever needed to be done. Closing his dresser drawers, he turned back to the bed. The pillows were fluffed and lined up against the headboard...he was positive that they would smell April fresh. This whole situation was becoming more and more surreal. He felt like he had the perfect wife...without any of the carnal benefits.

Groaning, he kicked off his shoes and padded into his bathroom. He stood in front of the mirror, staring at his own reflection. Out of the corner of his eyes, he caught sight of her. She was lounging in his big tub, covered in bubbles up to her chin, her hair pinned up on top of her head. One sexy foot peeked out of the water at the edge of the tub. When she smiled, his gut tightened and blood rushed to his groin. He turned slowly, then blinked. The bathtub was empty with no sign of having been used anytime recently. Scowling, he cursed loudly and stomped from the room.

Val fell into a comfortable schedule that ended up keeping her out of George's sight for most of the weekdays. She often baked goodies for him to take to his parents on Sundays, but never joined them for the weekly meal. However, she continued to cook great dinners and fill the house with freshly made and baked goodies.

Nearing the middle of October, George approached Val for help. She was in the kitchen, washing dishes.

"Val?"

"Yeah?"

He leaned against the counter next to her and folded his arms across his chest. "Can I ask you a favor?"

"Sure," she answered without looking up.

"Halloween is quickly approaching," he started.

"All hallow's eve."

Nodding, he glanced sideways at her. "I usually buy Jess a costume to wear...some Disney character or what-have-you."

She rinsed a dish and placed it on the drain rack. "And this year?"

He blew out a breath, "She wants to be a pink ballerina."

Val grinned at the tone of his voice, "I'd be happy to help."

"I looked in the stores and they have ballerina costumes, but they aren't pink," he complained.

"We'll have to improvise, then."

He nodded, "Thanks."

"No problem."

"Is everything going all right for you?" he asked suddenly.

"Sure. Why?"

"Just thought I'd check in...make sure you have everything you need and all."

She dried her hands on the dishtowel before hanging it up, "Everything is fine."

"Need any time off? Want to go home to visit Robyn?"

Frowning, she turned to face him, "Is there a problem?"

"No!" he exclaimed. "You're just so quiet and you never seem to ask for anything. I wanted to make sure you were happy...content."

She stared at him for a moment, wanting to tell him the truth. She had asked him to be honest with her at all times...but could she do the same? "I'm fine. Everything is great."

"You'll tell me if you need anything, right?"

"Of course."

He eyed her for a moment, "I'm, uh, taking Jess to my parents' house on Saturday to stay overnight."

"Okay. I'll make sure she has a bag packed," she responded.

"Great," he shifted and looked over her shoulder. "Would you, uh, like to have dinner out Saturday night? With me?"

"What?"

"I thought it would be nice to have an adult night out while Jess was otherwise occupied," he suggested.

"Just the two of us?" she asked incredulously.

"Sure. We'll have a nice quiet dinner. I can even find a show to go see, if you'd like."

A date. She shivered and bit her lip. Alone with George for a whole evening. She should thank him politely for the offer and then decline. "All right. Sounds like fun."

He brightened and pushed away from the counter. "Great. I'll

TRUTH AND LIES
================

take care of everything."
  She frowned as he walked away. He was that kind of guy...take
charge, take care of everything. Fortunately, this was only one
harmless night out. Leaving the kitchen, she mentally reviewed the
clothes in her closet. There had to be something in there she could
wear.

  Val packed the last item in Jessica's tiny pink suitcase. "All ready!"
Jess hopped from one foot to the other. "Nana and I always make
fun things."
  "I bet you do."
  "And I get to sleep in the blue room."
  "Quite a change from your bedroom, huh?" Val teased as George
appeared in the doorway.
  "Time to go, sweets."
  Val stood and held out the suitcase for him, "George?"
  He stepped aside as Jess skipped out of her room, "Yes?"
  "My turn to ask a favor."
  "Sure."
  She blushed and tapped her short fingernail against the dresser.
"May I use your bathtub?"
  He froze in the doorway, half turned away from her, "Oh, uh,
sure."
  "I won't take long...I just love Jacuzzi tubs," she explained.
  "No problem. Take as long as you like," he offered, backing out
of the pink bedroom. "Enjoy."
  "Great, thanks."
  "I'll be back in a little while."
  She nodded and watched him hurry away. Back in her room, she
gathered a robe, some bubble bath and her toiletries. Armed with her
supplies, she strode down the hall to his room. As usual, his bathroom
was sparkling clean and extremely tidy. Locking the bathroom door,
she started the water in the tub and began to undress.
  When the tub was about half full, she started the Jacuzzi jets and
poured in a capful of bubble bath. Folding her dirty clothes, she placed

63

them neatly next to the sink. When she turned back to the tub, she smiled in delight. It looked soothing and decadent and she couldn't wait to get in! Turning off the water, she sat down on the edge of the tub and swung her legs over. She sank down slowly into the hot water, sighing as the bubbles caressed her skin. This was heaven. She leaned her head back and closed her eyes. Even the sound of the jets in the tub seemed distant and relaxing. She could do this every day.

She had no idea how long she had been in the tub when her eyes popped open. Was that a noise in the bedroom? The bathroom door was locked, but how much protection was that? After all, it was way too soon for George to have returned, wasn't it? She sank deeper into the warm water until the bubbles touched her chin. Oh, there it was again!

"Val?"

"It was him...George! He was tapping on the bathroom door!"

"Yeah?"

"I'm back. But take your time, okay?" he called over the sound of the jets.

"Okay," she paused, "George?"

"Yeah?"

"What time do we have to leave?"

"Six."

"Okay."

"George?"

He closed his eyes when she called his name again. "Yes?"

"What time is it now?"

She had to be naked...in his bathroom...in his tub...in steaming hot water that would lap at her curves. "Four-thirty."

"Okay, thanks."

He nodded to no one in particular and sagged against the bathroom door. He'd pictured her in his tub before, but this was worse. Now he *knew* she'd been in his tub...without her clothes. He couldn't breathe. Pushing away from the door, he crossed to his closet and pulled out some clothes for the evening. He had absolutely no reason to be in the bedroom at that moment but he couldn't tear himself away. When he heard the Jacuzzi jets turn off a few minutes later, he held his breath. She would stand up and water would slide down her body, leaving her slick and clean. The air would be cold on her skin so her nipples would pucker in response. He dragged in a deep breath, the blood rushing through his veins at an alarming speed. Wanting to break down the door between them, instead he shoved his hands in his pockets and left the room.

Downstairs he made himself some coffee and hid in the kitchen. He was horribly aroused...to the point where it was almost painful. He hadn't felt like this in years, not since Bernice. That in itself was a sobering thought. Val was nothing like Bernice and he was a totally different person now but the attraction was similar. He wanted Val with a white-hot passion but she was off-limits for many reasons, including her own recent divorce.

He could hear her walking around overhead. Hopefully she would be back in her bedroom, dressed in some long, shroud-like clothing. Somehow he would get through this evening without touching her. He would see her, smell her, want her...but he would keep his hands to himself.

He looked great, he smelled good...she wanted to just eat him up. How could he sit there, looking so fine, and not notice her lolling tongue? Shaking her head, she tried to concentrate on the show. At this point she had absolutely no idea what was going on. All she really knew was that his shoulders were too broad for these seats and he was constantly brushing up against her. His suit jacket was rough against her bare shoulder and she shivered.

"Are you cold?" he whispered into her ear.

"A little," she murmured back.

He wasn't surprised. She was wearing a clingy green sleeveless dress that left her beautiful arms and shoulders bare. Leaning forward, he pulling off his jacket, then settled it around her shoulders.

"Thank you," she said softly, pulling the coat tight around her.

Closing her eyes, she inhaled quietly. His scent surrounded her, wafting up from the dark gray fabric.

"Better?"

She nodded and leaned back in her seat. She could pretend, for just this one night, that he was hers. Unconsciously, she leaned toward him, wanting to feel his body touching hers. In response, he shifted and draped his arm around her back.

When the lights came up at intermission, she blinked and turned to look at him. His eyes were dark and focused on her mouth. "George?"

He grunted and shifted his gaze to hers. "Yeah?"

"Are you all right?" she whispered.

"Can we get out of here?"

She studied him. "Are you feeling okay?"

"Yeah." Leaning over, he put his face only inches from hers, "Lets get out of here."

"Okay."

They stood and slipped from their seats. Once in the aisle, they linked hands and made their way to the lobby. Outside the night air was cool as they hurried to the car. The ride home was made in complete silence and once inside the house, they stood in the foyer and stared at each other.

"Val..." he reached to touch the soft curl resting on her shoulder.

She took a step toward him. "What are we doing?"

Framing her face with his hands, he stepped closer. "Lets not ask, okay?"

She was mesmerized by his deep brown eyes. When he lowered his mouth to hers, her eyes fluttered closed. The moment his lips touched hers, her heart stopped. He brushed his mouth over hers, softly, then kissed her tenderly. She never knew that a kiss could be so soft and yet so terribly arousing. Without thinking, she moved forward, pressing herself against him.

George smoothed his hands down her throat and then lower to push his coat from her shoulders. Her skin glowed in the semi-darkness and he leaned over to press a kiss to her newly bared flesh. She was warm and silky under his lips. Groaning, he felt her fingers push through his hair. "Val..."

She gasped and let his tongue plunder her mouth. He was hot and wet but his touch was tender. She'd never had a man worship her quite like this before. She could feel each of his fingertips as he caressed her arms.

Moving his hands down her arms to her hands, he tugged her with him into the dark family room. Dropping onto the couch, he pulled her onto his lap and moaned as he felt the imprint of her body on his. Capturing her face again, he kissed her with all the longing in his soul. She was sweet and sexy and he wanted nothing more than to enjoy her all night. He wanted her naked body pressed against his in the dark solitude of his bedroom. Dragging the strap of her dress down her arm, he bared new flesh. With a groan, he kissed her there.

Chills raced up her spine as she felt his tongue sweep across her shoulder to the hollow of her throat. The only sounds in the room were their breathing and the sound of lips meeting flesh. "George..."

"Valerie..." he growled. "Come to bed with me."

She moaned and slid from his lap. When he stood next to her, she leaned into his big, hard body. They stood motionless like that for a moment, feeling the beating of their hearts. Pulling away in a trance, she turned toward the hallway to the stairs. With a startled gasp, she tripped over a box on the floor. As they stood in stunned silence, crayons scattered across the carpet.

"Val," his voice was low and husky with desire. "Don't..."

Covering her mouth, she shook her head. What was she doing? She must have lost her mind. Without another word, she turned and scurried from the room.

He groaned and rubbed a hand over his face. What had just happened here? He knelt on the floor and collected the runaway crayons. Once they were back in their box, he set them on the coffee table. Resting back on his heels, he stared out in the empty foyer. He could still taste her...if he inhaled, he could still smell her. His body was more than ready to complete the evening's activities but his mind was in utter turmoil. He wanted her...more than he had *ever* wanted Bernice. He could easily lose his head over this woman...as had almost happened tonight. But did he really know her? Was the woman now living in his house, caring for his daughter, the real Valerie? It wouldn't be wise to rush into anything with her, even though she was right under his nose twenty-four hours a day.

Man, how was he going to restrain himself? Now that he knew the taste and feel of her, how was he going to keep his hands and mouth to himself? Overhead he could hear her moving around. She was probably stripping off her dress and sliding into bed. Groaning, he got to his feet and retrieved his jacket from the foyer floor. He knew her scent lingered on the material and he resisted pulling it to his nose to absorb her smell.

Val lay back in bed, her eyes open and fixed on the ceiling. She had lost her mind that was all there was to it. How could she have let this happen? Touching a trembling finger to her throbbing lips, she swallowed back tears. She'd never been kissed so tenderly before.

Sex with Craig had always been fun and exciting...sometimes even acrobatic...but never soft and sensuous. She had a feeling that soft and sensuous was George's forte. Huddling under her covers, she heard footsteps ascending the stairs. She froze when the footsteps paused outside her door, then released a breath when they finally continued down the hall to George's room. Straining, she heard his door close softly.

How was she going to face him tomorrow? Fortunately for her, he would be going to Sunday dinner at his parents house and she could cower at home alone. Maybe she should just go home. With a soft cry, she realized that she didn't have a home to go to. She had already signed a contract on the house. By the end of the month, it would have new owners. No matter what, she would have to make this situation with George and Jessica work.

Chapter
Seven

After hiding in her room most of Sunday, Val came up with a new schedule for her daily life. Starting Monday morning, she began staying in her bedroom until it was time to wake Jessica. Then, once Jess was ready, the two of them went downstairs to have breakfast. Within twenty minutes of their appearance, George would leave for work and Val could relax for a few hours. She did her daily chores, went grocery shopping and prepared dinner. Sitting through dinner with George across the table was tense, but once dinner was over George and Jess left her alone in the kitchen to clean up. Shortly thereafter, she went outside to take a walk around the neighborhood. The exercise was both for fitness and to release the tension from dinner. By the time she returned from her walk, George and Jess were engrossed in bath-time and Val was able to sneak away into her bedroom to hide.

On the surface, nothing seemed to have changed but there were a few differences. She couldn't force herself to enter George's bedroom to make his bed or gather his laundry. Just the thought of touching his sheets and smelling him was enough to send shivers through her entire being.

And so her routine was set. She and George were never alone and they never discussed what happened. It was Halloween before they were required to really confront each other at all.

"I want Val to come with," Jess said, plaintively.

George knelt in front of his pink ballerina. "I'm going trick or treating with you."

"I want Val to come, too."

"I have to stay here and give out candy to the other children in the neighborhood," Val explained.

"Can't you just leave the candy on the porch?" Jess asked.

Val laughed softly. "No, honey. Now you go with Daddy and have a fun time. And remember what you tell people when they ask who you are."

"I'm the pink fairy. I bring the love of pink to everyone's heart," she repeated dutifully. She was wearing a pink leotard, pink tights, a pink tutu and pink ballerina slippers. Val had found a tin foil tiara and star-topped wand that she had spray-painted pink.

"Good! Now go get your candy," Val instructed with a false smile.

Jess turned away and took her father's hand. As they headed for the door, she looked over her tiny shoulder at Val, giving her a sad little look.

Val wriggled her fingers in a cheery wave. When they were finally out the door, she slumped down onto the sofa. She was becoming terribly attached to that little girl.

Val was sitting in almost exactly the same position when George and Jess reappeared just over an hour later. Jess was propped in her father's arms, a bag of candy clutched in her hands.

"All done?"

George nodded and closed the door behind him. He started down the hall toward the stairs when Jess called out for Valerie.

"I want Val to tuck me in."

Val blinked in surprise. Bedtime was a special time for father and daughter and she had made certain to stay out of the way. "Daddy will tuck you in."

"No!" Jess practically howled. "I want Val!"

Val could almost feel the hurt radiating off George as she took Jess into her arms. She couldn't meet his gaze as Jess snuggled against her. Carrying her up the stairs and into her room, she set Jess on her bed. "Did you have fun tonight?"

Jess nodded tiredly, allowing Val to strip off her costume. "I got lots of candy."

"I bet you did." Val tossed the ballerina outfit into the laundry basket. "And you were a beautiful pink fairy." She swung Jess' legs up onto the bed and pulled the sheet up over her.

"Val?"

"Yes, sweetie?"

"I love you," Jess murmured, her eyes already closed.

Tears formed in the back of her throat as she brushed Jess' hair away from her face. "I love you, too, Jess."

In the hallway, hidden in the shadows, George frowned. It was hard for him to share his daughter's affections like this. Having Val in their lives twenty-four hours a day had really changed things. No matter what she thought, she was now a member of their family. Spinning away, he went back downstairs to give out more candy.

"It's almost my birthday!" Jess sang as she skipped into the kitchen.

Val followed her into the kitchen carrying a bag of cupcake supplies. Jess' preschool teacher had approved her request to bring cupcakes to the children for Jess' birthday. Now all they had to do was make them.

Without even being told, Jess went directly to the sink to wash her hands. "My birthday, my birthday!" she continued to sing.

Grinning, Val unloaded the bags and set out two muffin pans on the kitchen table. She instructed Jess on how to place the paper cupcake wrappers into the muffin tins. While she was doing that, Val started making the cupcake batter.

"Nana is making me a party this weekend," Jess said, happily as she peeled apart the cupcake wrappers.

"And what do you want for your birthday, little miss?" Val asked.

"A dog," she answered promptly.

"And have you told Daddy about that?"

"Of course," her voice was matter-of-fact.

"And what did he say?"

Jess frowned as she continued to pull the wrappers apart and set them on the table. "He says, no."

"So what else do you want?"

"Pink gloves."

Val nodded and brought the cupcake batter to the table. "For when it snows."

"And when it's cold, too." She watched as Val poured batter into the prepared muffin tins, "When is your birthday?"

"March."

"Daddy's birthday is in July," Jess propped her tiny chin in her hand. "Will you have a party for your birthday?"

"Maybe." Val hedged before changing the subject. "Lets put these cupcakes in the oven and start the frosting, okay?"

"When do we get to put the sprinkles on?"

"After we put the frosting on," Val answered. "Why don't you pour the sprinkles into that little bowl?"

Jess opened the jar of sprinkles and dumped them into the bowl. "How do we get the sprinkles onto the cupcakes?"

"We're going to turn the cupcakes upside and push them into the sprinkles."

"What if we squash the cupcake?" Jess' eyes were wide with concern.

"We'll have to be very careful. And if we still squash one, then we'll eat it!" she grinned as Jess giggled with delight.

"Robyn, what am I going to do?" Val practically whispered into the phone. George and Jess were at Jess' birthday party.

Robyn's sigh could be heard over the telephone line. "What are your choices, really?"

"I don't have very many choices at all," she moaned. "I don't want a man in my life. I don't want someone else taking care of everything for me."

"It was only a kiss, right? And he doesn't seem any more interested in talking about it than you are," Robyn told her. "Maybe he figured it was a mistake, too. Maybe you should just put it out of your mind...forget about it."

Groaning, Val closed her eyes. "I'm not sure I can just forget it."

"That good, huh?"

"You know that my sex life with Craig was good," Val began, "I can't really complain about that. But what George did to me that night...oh man."

"Val! You said it was just a kiss!" Robyn gasped.

"It was!" Val assured her. "But it was like he was making love to my mouth. It was warm and soft and...oh lord, Robyn! I've never been kissed quite like that." She touched a finger to her lips. "I can't even look him in the face anymore. All I see is the expression that he had that night."

"And you're sure that this is something you don't want to pursue? George is a great guy," Robyn reminded her.

"I'm here to care for Jess. She has to be my priority. What if I did get involved with George and for some reason it didn't last? How could I hurt this little girl like that?"

Sighing, Robyn agreed with her. "You're right, Jess comes first. I hate to say it, but maybe you and George need to talk about this."

"I can't...I just can't face him."

Val was jerked from sleep at a sound coming from her bedroom door. She slipped out of bed and opened the door to find Jessica standing in the hallway, still in her pajamas. "Sweetie, what are you doing awake?"

"I'm scared," she lisped around her thumb.

Val picked her up and retreated into her own bedroom, closing the door behind her. "What are you scared of, honey?" She sank down onto the bed and cradled the little girl in her arms.

"Tom," she whispered.

"Who is Tom? Is he a boy in your class?" Val rubbed her back soothingly.

"Tom the Turkey."

She wanted to laugh, but instead pressed a kiss to Jess' temple. "Did you read about Tom in school?"

Jess nodded against Val's chest.

"Why are you afraid of Tom?" Val wanted to know.

"He's going to gobble gobble me up."

If there hadn't been tears in her quivering voice, Val would have grinned. "Where did you hear that?"

"Teacher said that's what he does. Gobble gobble," She repeated before pressing her face into Val's neck, tears streaming down her face.

Val knew she would have to talk to Miss Lynn, Jess' preschool teacher. But for now, the best she could do was reassure Jess. "Tom can't get in the house, sweetie."

She just continued to cry and clutch at Val.

"Why don't you sleep in here with me tonight, okay?" Val stretched out on her queen sized bed and pulled Jess against her. "I'll stay right here with you."

Sniffling, Jess snuggled up against Val and hiccuped softly, "You won't leave?"

Val rubbed her arm reassuringly. "I'll be right here. Go back to sleep." As Jess drifted off, Val felt her heart contract. This precious little girl was definitely a permanent part of her heart.

Even after Val had spoken to Miss Lynn, Jess continued to have nightmares about Tom the Turkey. It was later in the month when George found out.

He was awakened from a sound sleep by a noise. By the time he got to Jess' room, Val was right on his heels. Jess was sitting up in bed, sobbing. He stooped and reached for her, but she had other ideas. She looked around him and put her arms out for Val. In shock, he stumbled and fell to his knees next to the little pink bed. His daughter was frightened or possibly hurt and she reached for a stranger for comfort.

Val shot him a look he couldn't read and scurried past him to reach for Jess. "Don't cry, baby," she soothed.

"What's wrong?" he asked, his voice raspy with hurt.

"It's Tom!" Jess wailed. "He's coming to get me!"

He stood, startled at the stark terror in his daughter's voice. "Tom, who?" he looked around, searching the darkness of her bedroom.

"Tom, the Thanksgiving day Turkey," Val murmured, rubbing Jess' back. "We've talked about this, honey. Tom can't get into the house."

"He was looking in the window!" Jess accused.

"You're all right, Jess, you're safe," Val reassured her.

"How long has this been going on?" he demanded.

"Only a week or two," Val whispered, holding Jess close. "This is the worst it's been."

"The turkey can't hurt you, Jess," he told his daughter.

"He's going to gobble gobble me up!" she sobbed harder.

Val glanced over at George who looked utterly lost and helpless. "Jess? Listen to me, sweets."

She sniffled and quieted.

"See how big and strong Daddy is?" Val whispered. "He's going to look around for Tom and scare him away."

Jess looked over at her father.

"Once Daddy is done, Tom won't want to come anywhere near you, okay?" Val turned to face George, who looked quite confused. "Here's your job. Check the closet, under the bed, behind the door...make sure Tom is nowhere to be found. And make sure he knows that you're here to protect Jess."

"The window, too, Daddy," Jess whispered.

He straightened to his full height and stalked to the closet. Throwing open the door, he began raking his hands through the clothes hanging there. "Are you hiding in the closet, Tom? You'd better not be because I'm here now and there's no way I'm going to let you near Jess." He closed the door and turned, "No Tom in there." Walking across the room, he knelt next to the bed and peered underneath. "You'd better not be hiding under here, either. I mean it, Tom, I'm here to stay and I'm way bigger than you." With the same loud voice, he continued around the room, repeating the same threats. When he was done, he turned back to his daughter who practically leapt from Val's arms into his.

"Oh, thank you, Daddy!" she cried, kissing him soundly.

He hugged her close as he met Val's gaze over her little blond head.

Val could see the gratitude in his eyes. She had restored a little girl's faith in her father and given him back his little girl's trust. Her eyes slid away from his as she slipped from the cotton candy room without another word. She was curled up on her side in her bed

75

when she heard tapping on her door. "Yes?"

"May I?" he called softly.

"Okay." She focused on his bare legs when the door opened. She knew he was clad only in shorts and a tee shirt.

"I just wanted to say thank you," he murmured.

"I should have told you sooner."

He shrugged and leaned against the doorframe. "You were handling it."

"She loves you, you know."

Nodding, he picked at the paint on the doorjamb. "It's just hard for me to share after four years of having her all to myself. It's hard to see her reach for someone else...it used to be me."

She was silent. There was nothing she could tell him to make him feel better.

"Well, good night," he murmured before turning away. Without any further comment, he shut the door between them.

Val hadn't moved during the conversation but now she rolled onto her back and stared at the ceiling. She'd had to pull on every ounce of energy she had to keep from reaching for him. His heat, his scent was imprinted on her brain and there was no escape. Robyn was right, they had to talk about this.

Chapter
Eight

"You will not be alone on Thanksgiving," George said from the kitchen doorway. "You might as well agree to come or I'll sic Robyn on you."

Val's shoulders were tight with tension. She was just finishing the strawberry shortcake she'd planned to send along with him and Jess.

"No more excuses, Val. Be ready to leave by four," he ordered before disappearing.

She cursed under her breath and covered the shortcake for the thirty-minute ride. Along with that she placed a fresh loaf of homemade pumpkin bread. With just two hours to get ready, she stomped upstairs to take a shower. She was looking forward to seeing Robyn and her family but nervous about George's parents. Without ever having met them, she was utterly intimidated. She wasn't sure how she fit in and was uncomfortable just thinking about it. After taking a quick shower, she dressed in a long skirt and sweater set before doing her hair. She took a light hand with her makeup before leaving her room. Back in the kitchen, she gathered up the bread and cake.

"Are you ready?"

She whirled around at the sound of his voice. "Yes."

He stood speechless in the doorway, his dark eyes raking over her womanly form. She was magnificent in red, brown and tan, covered from neck to almost feet. His heart thundered in his chest and his mouth went dry. Her sweater clung to her curves and flowed into a long soft skirt that slid over her hips and feel in graceful waves to her ankles. "What....," his voice cracked. "What has to go?"

"Just these," she indicated her two packages.

Stepping forward, he relieved her of her parcels and turned away. "Jess! Lets go!"

Jessica was waiting for them in the front foyer. "Is Val coming with?"

"Yes, she is," he answered, propelling his daughter out the front door to the minivan. "And she's going to have a great time."

Val grunted and stuck her tongue out at his back.

"I'm glad. I don't like it when we leave you home alone," Jess stated.

"I'm alone all the time, sweets," Val told her as she climbed into the minivan. "It's okay to be alone sometimes."

"I don't like to be alone," Jess said after Val settled into her own seat. "It's no fun."

"Well, we're going to have fun today!" George interrupted. "Aunt Robyn, Uncle Erik and your cousin Maddie are all waiting for us at Nana and Paw-Paw's."

"And we get to have ham for dinner!" Jess enthused.

Val smiled silently. After all the turkey nightmares, she wasn't surprised to find the main dish was a pig instead. Evidently pigs are non-threatening.

"And chicken. And stuffing. And cornbread," he listed. "Possibly pie, certainly cake." He was referring to Val's contribution. "You have no idea how fat you've made my dad."

"Paw-Paw says he's jolly," Jess spoke up from the back seat.

"Santa Claus is jolly...Paw-Paw is just fat," he teased. "All those cakes and pies and breads."

"Paw-Paw is all soft like a big teddy bear."

"He's hairy like a bear, too."

"Dad-dy!" Jess called. "He is not!"

Val listened to the two of them, hoping that Paw-Paw liked her half as much as he liked her baking.

"Stop worrying," George hissed to her as they strode up the front walk.

"I'm not worried," Val said blithely.

He grunted and allowed Jessica to open the front door. "Mom, Dad, we're here!" Indicating for Val to precede him into the house, he waited for the stampede. Within seconds, they heard footsteps clattering down the hall.

"Nana, Paw-Paw!" Jess exclaimed, skipping ahead to throw herself into her grandmother's arms.

"Hello there, sweetie," Marcy Richards scooped Jess into her embrace. Hefting the child up into her arms, she stepped forward to kiss George's cheek. "Hi, honey."

"Hi, Mom. Hi, Pop," he greeted them.

"And this must be the queen of cakes!" Ed Richards stepped up to Val and engulfed her in a hug. "God bless you, child!"

Val couldn't help but grin and hug him back, "Nice to meet you." She could see how Erik was the spitting image of his father. Ed was well-built like Erik, but his hair was speckled with gray and his eyes held years of understanding. She liked him right away and felt comfortable in his presence. He reminded her of several of her foster fathers...down-to-earth and just plain kind. While he was clean and dressed nicely, there was still a rumpled look about him that reminded her of warmth and home. Marcy, on the other hand, was tall and regal and looked more like she was ready for a cotillion. It was easy to see that she was used to dressing well, no matter what the occasion, and that she valued being well put together. Her skirt and blouse were crisply ironed, her hair was perfectly styled and her makeup was impeccably applied. Val could see where George had gotten his good looks as his face was a masculine version of Marcy's. All in all, they seemed like nice people though she was a little intimidated by Marcy. Even in her favorite skirt and sweater, she felt disheveled and unkempt next to George's mother. She had the urge to run to the powder room to check her hair and makeup.

"Come on back," Marcy called cheerfully. "The rest of the crew is in the kitchen, as usual."

"We're so glad you could join us, Valerie." Ed wrapped his arm around her waist and guided her down the hallway.

"Val made cake," Jess announced from her position in Marcy's arms.

Ed squeezed her closer. "Darlin', if I wasn't already married..."

"Oh, Ed, stop that," Marcy admonished. "You'll scare that poor child away."

"Val!" Robyn squealed from the table. "Come hug me," she demanded.

Val grinned and hugged her pregnant friend. "You look great!" Robyn was wearing a peach colored dress that showed off her pregnant belly.

"Val! Val! Val!" Maddie chanted from her booster seat.

"Hi, hi, hi!" Val called back, hugging the little cherub. "How was your trip?" Leaning over, she kissed Erik's cheek.

He grinned and dragged her into his lap. "It was great. But seeing you is even better."

Val giggled and swung her legs back and forth. "You're as cute as ever."

Sticking his tongue out at his wife, he crowed, "At least someone still thinks I'm cute."

"Da! Cute! Da! Cute!" Maddie chanted happily.

"Thank you, munchkin," he pressed a kiss to her chubby little cheek.

"Enough!" Robyn called, laughing. "You'll give him a swelled head."

George watched this whole scene in silence. He was interested to see how differently Val was acting in the company of her friends. He was also interested to see how cozy she was in his brother's lap.

Jess skipped around the table and reached out to Val. "I want to sit with you, too."

Val grinned at Erik before lifting Jess onto her lap.

"Ugh," he grunted as she wriggled around to get comfortable. "Jess, little girl, you've grown."

She giggled and pursed her lips for a kiss.

Erik obliged, giving her a noisy, wet kiss.

"Hey, me too," Robyn said from the other side of Maddie.

With a moan, he leaned over and kissed his wife. Lifting an eyebrow, he glared at George. "Anyone else?"

"Give it a couple of months and there will be one more," Val teased, eyeing Robyn's bulging stomach.

"If I don't pass out from hunger first," Robyn complained.

Erik nudged his lap occupants. "That's my cue to feed Mama."

Jess and Val vacated his lap in favor of their own chairs.

"There's a platter of cheese and crackers in the fridge, honey," Marcy said from the stove. "George, honey, would you pull out the ham so I can baste it?"

He did so, keeping his facial expression neutral. Val seemed at ease with his family, which made him wonder even more at her reluctance to come to previous dinners.

"So," Ed rubbed his hands together almost gleefully. "What goodies did you bring us, Val?"

"I, uh, brought strawberry shortcake and a loaf of pumpkin bread," she told him.

"Oh boy! How will I ever have enough room to eat everything tonight?" he laughed.

"Somehow you'll survive, dear," Marcy said wryly. With a wave, she instructed George to return the ham to the oven. "We should be ready to eat in about forty minutes."

"Can I help with anything?" Val asked tentatively.

"No, no, we're all done with everything. Does anyone want a drink?" she offered, nudging her husband.

"Right, drinks! Erik, scotch?" he went to the cabinet to retrieve some glasses.

"Sure, Pop," he answered absently, feeding a cracker to his wife, then his daughter.

"George?" Ed held up the bottle.

"No, thanks," he shook his head. He wasn't much of a drinker and preferred not to imbibe when he had to drive home.

"Val, what can I get you?" Ed wanted to know.

Her eyes flitted to George's face, then slid away. "Just some water would be great."

"No scotch with that water?" he teased, filling a glass with ice and water.

She just smiled and accepted the tumbler.

"So, Val, how do you like watching my grandbaby?" Marcy asked, stroking Jess' blond hair.

"She's an absolute delight," Val enthused. "She's very bright and just soaks up new things like a little sponge."

"I'm not a sponge!" Jess protested with a frown.

"I'm sorry, sweetie. You're a wonderful student who loves to learn," Val corrected herself.

Jess nodded in acknowledgment.

"She certainly got her father's intelligence," Marcy commented.

"It's a good thing that she got her momma's looks," Erik said jovially. After a moment of stunned silence, he shot his brother an apologetic look.

Val ran a hand over Jess' silky blond hair. "Yes, she did."

Jess looked around at the quiet adults, then shrugged. "Val, want to see the blue room where I sleep?"

"Sure." She stood.

"Blue woom," Maddie cried, holding out her arms to Val.

Grinning, Val picked up the toddler and set her on her hip. "Anyone else want to see the blue woom?" When no one would meet her gaze, she turned and followed Jess from the room.

"George," Marcy hissed. "Go with her."

Erik rolled his eyes. "Ma..."

George glared at his mother, then did as he was told and followed the trio upstairs to the guest bedroom.

"I like to stay here," Jess was saying. When she spotted her father in the doorway, she called out. "Can I stay here tonight, Daddy?"

"Nana already has company tonight, sweets," he told her, staying just outside the room.

"Please...," she begged, clutching his hand in hers. "Can I ask Nana?"

He frowned and looked over at Val, but she refused to meet his gaze. "Not this time."

Her lower lip poked out and tears welled up in her eyes. "But I love the blue room."

"Jessica!" he said sternly.

At the sound of his voice, Maddie jerked in Val's arms and began crying. Val swung away and shushed the little girl. She was loathe to correct George in front of his daughter, but what was the big deal? If Marcy didn't want Jess, she was sure she would say so. Jiggling Maddie in her arms, she walked over to the curtained window.

"Daddy..." Jess whispered tearfully. "I want to stay here with Nana and Paw-Paw."

Taking her hand, he led her out of the room.

Val couldn't hear what they were saying but the realization suddenly hit her. If Jess stayed here, then she and George would be going home alone. Good Lord, was that why he was so upset? After a few minutes of soothing murmurs, Maddie settled down and they left the blue room. Back in the kitchen she found Jess huddled in Ed's arms.

"Don't be ridiculous, George," Marcy said. "We have plenty of room. And it will be nice for Maddie and Jess to be able to spend time together."

Jess sniffled and shot her father a look of triumph.

Val's eyes widened and flew first to George's face, then to Robyn's.

"Val!" Robyn said loudly. "Why don't you come help me change for dinner." Standing, she crossed the room and grabbed Val's arm.

"Why are you changing for dinner?" Erik asked in confusion.

Robyn glared at her husband before depositing their daughter in his lap. "We'll be right back," she said to Marcy before dragging Val upstairs. When they reached the bedroom where Erik and Robyn had settled in earlier, she closed the door.

Val crossed the room and plopped onto the bed. "They're letting her stay, aren't they?"

"Yeah," Robyn whispered, watching Val cautiously.

"What am I going to do?"

"I don't know." Robyn leaned against the door. "Maybe you'll both be so exhausted..."

Val closed her eyes, groaning loudly. "If he touches me, I'm in big trouble."

"Maybe he won't."

"God, Robyn...if he even looks at me funny, I know I'll just melt," Val complained.

"Maybe you should just let it happen," she suggested softly. "You might enjoy it."

"And maybe I could just spontaneously combust," Val said wryly.

George stood impatiently next to the front door as Val said her good-byes.

"We're so glad you came," Marcy said, releasing her from a hug.

"Thank you for having me...and for the wonderful meal," Val responded.

"See you tomorrow evening for leftovers," Robyn murmured, hugging her tightly. "Good luck," she whispered softly in Val's ear.

Val rolled her eyes and pulled back. When she turned to leave, she found George watching her closely. "Good night, all."

George let her walk past him then he turned to follow. At the last minute, Erik grabbed his arm. "Yes?"

"Don't hurt her," Erik said very very softly.

George just grunted and pulled away. "See you tomorrow night." He followed Val out to the van and got in without any comment.

They were halfway home before Val spoke. "Thank you for taking me tonight."

He nodded, but kept his eyes on the road.

"George?"

"What?"

She cringed at his harsh response. "Are we going to talk about this?"

"About what?"

Frowning in the darkness, she wondered if he was going to make this difficult for her. "This thing between us."

"There's nothing to talk about."

Pressing her lips together, she fell back into silence. When they pulled up in front of the house, she hopped out of the van and strode up to the front door. Without waiting for him, she unlocked the door and went inside.

Angry with her and with himself, he followed her inside. He caught up with her on the stairs and grabbed her arm. "What do you want from me?"

"Nothing," she tried to shake him off, but he held on.

With one step he was pressing her against the wall. "Then why do I want so much from you?" he growled before lowering his head.

"George…," she whispered, eyes wide.

"No talk, Valerie," he muttered. "Just action." With that, he kissed her.

Her eyes slammed shut at the touch of his mouth on hers. She was immediately on fire for him. Sliding her hands up his chest, she wrapped her arms around his neck and hung on. She moaned as his tongue thrust past her lips to explore her mouth.

He wanted her…she was under his skin, in his soul and he wanted her. This time he would not let her go. Stooping slightly, he swept her up in his arms and thumped up the stairs. The hallway was dark but he didn't really notice. Once inside his bedroom, he set her gently on her feet. "Val…"

She didn't want to think about anything but his touch. With trembling hands, she began unbuttoning his shirt. As she did, he reached for her sweater. Then they were gasping and pulling at each other's clothes.

He walked her backwards toward the bed, each of them clad only in their underwear. "Val…"

Smiling, she reached up to caress his face. "I've imagined this moment…even wished for it some nights," she whispered.

"And now?"

"And now I'm wondering what the hell we're waiting for."

Chapter
Nine

He grinned in the darkness and gently lowered her to the bed. Kneeling on one knee next to her, he kissed her slowly and thoroughly. While his mouth was busy, so were his hands. He rolled onto his back, bringing her on top of him. From that position it was easy to relieve her of her bra.

She smiled down at him, arching to assist him. Her smile turned to a moan when he touched her sensitized flesh.

"You're beautiful, Val," he murmured before taking one already engorged peak into his mouth. She was firm, full and sweet between his lips. He flicked her nipple with his tongue and groaned in reaction to her guttural response. Aching to be inside her, he rolled again, pinning her beneath him. Where Bernice had been all angles and sharp bones, Val was soft, rounded curves.

She clutched at his shoulder, digging her fingers and short nails into his flesh. "Do that again, George," she begged, pushing her hands into his mink brown hair and holding him to her breast.

He obliged, using slow manipulations to torture her. She responded incredibly to his every touch. Lifting his head, he met her gaze. "Val...I have to get up."

She shook her head mutely and pulled him down to kiss her. With a quick gasp of air, she sucked his lower lip into her mouth and laved it with her tongue.

Grunting, he felt light-headed when all the blood in his head rushed to his groin. He jerked back and sucked in deep breaths to try and steady his pounding heart. "Valerie, honey...," he panted, framing her face with his hands. "Keep that thought."

"No, no, no," she chanted, grasping his slick flesh.

"I have to get some protection, Val. It's in the bathroom," he told

87

RIDA ALLEN

her gruffly.

She wrapped her legs around his hips and ground herself against him for a moment. Leaning forward, she nipped at his earlobe. "You keep that thought, George," was her hoarsely muttered demand.

He groaned and slipped from her embrace to stride quickly into the bathroom.

Grinning, she listened to him bang the cabinet doors looking for the condoms. It was a few minutes before she heard him make a triumphant noise and reappear.

"I was about ready to panic," he muttered, dropping the box onto his night stand. "Now," he stood over her. "Where were we?"

She reached for him, pulling him down on top of her. The sparse hair sprinkled across his broad chest rubbed across her nipples, making her gasp sharply. When he settled himself on top of her, she felt the need to burrow into his arms. Oh yes, she wanted him...but deep down there was another pull she refused to identify.

He touched his lips to hers, moving slowly, softly, wanting to enjoy every second he had. Her eyes were squeezed shut and he could feel the imprint of each of her fingers on his shoulders. Pressing kisses along her jaw and down her neck, he arched his pelvis and felt her welcoming heat through the remaining layers of underwear.

Arching her head back, she allowed him greater access to her throat. She moaned in pleasure and slid her hands down his back and under the waistband of his boxer briefs to grasp his buttocks. They were smooth and firm...like most of the rest of him.

He stood suddenly, almost wrenching himself from her grasp. With impatient hands, he stripped her of her panties, then shucked his own briefs.

Val watched in fascination as he stood tall and proud next to the bed. His broad chest narrowed only slightly to his tight stomach and hips. His legs were long and muscled, covered in dark curly hair that she itched to run her fingers through. And then there...he was beautiful. His manhood jutted out from his body, a smooth and strong muscle that made her want to kneel and worship him. What she did was scoot to the edge of the bed and reach for the condom packet in his

88

hand.

He released the foil packet, his eyes intent on the expression on her face. She seemed mesmerized as she reached out to touch him. With a groan, he jerked under the touch of her hand. "Val..."

Her liquid green gaze met his. "Shh...." She replaced her hands with her mouth and lips...lavishing attention on him. He throbbed wildly under her tongue.

"Val...," he grasped her shoulders and squeezed gently.

She released him slowly, then tore open the condom wrapper. With a few wayward caresses, she rolled on the protection, then looked up into his eyes. "Join me on the bed, George."

He did, catching her in his arms and pulling her close. She was warm and pliant under his hands. He kissed her, thrusting his tongue into her waiting mouth and sweeping across her tongue. His hands found her breasts and cupped them reverently. Lowering his head, he suckled at one breast while his fingers rolled and pinched the other nipple.

She arched up into his mouth, writhing her body beneath his. She was ready for him, no question, but was enjoying his attention. His hands were firm but gentle wherever he touched her and each spot was left to throb with pleasure. When she felt his hand caress her heated center, she cried out.

"You're so wet," he breathed, his mouth returning to hers. "I want to be inside you."

"George?"

"Yeah?"

"What the hell are you waiting for?" she whispered back.

He groaned and kissed her sassy mouth. Grasping her hips in his hands, he positioned himself in between her legs. When she wrapped her full, sexy legs around his waist, his manhood jerked against her moist opening.

Arching her hips, she waited for the hard thrust that would make them one. When he dipped inside slowly, she cried out and clutched at his shoulders. "George, please!"

He chuckled and held her hips tightly so that she couldn't rush the union. "Patience," he murmured, sliding in just a bit further. He could feel her warmth clinging to him as he eased slowly into her. With a final push, he filled her.

Sighing, she clenched her legs around him and rocked her hips toward him. He stretched her, making her feel as if he were touching every part of her. When he began moving with long, slow strokes, she moaned. She'd never been loved like this. Every second was worth cherishing, every move reverberating through her. She was accustomed to fast and furious, which could be exhilarating and terribly arousing, but often left her feeling incomplete. This...what he was doing to her...this was not only arousing, but it was intoxicating. He was focused entirely on her, on filling her up so that she could think of nothing else. She purred when his mouth found the hollow of her throat.

He could have shot off into space...that was how good he was feeling. With her arms wrapped around his neck, he was free to insinuate his hand between them. At her cry of pleasure, he groaned loudly and circled the protruding nub with his fingers. She was so sensitive...at each brush of his fingers over that tiny bundle of nerves, her insides clenched at him.

She was surprised at the way he played her, like a fine and valued instrument. Somehow he noted every gasp of air, every hitch of her breath, and responded appropriately. He seemed to know better what she wanted than she did! When he touched her again, then slid home, she exhaled on a cry and let herself go. She soared, her thighs quivering, her heart pounding and her insides exploding with pleasure.

He continued to stroke her as she climaxed, his own body taught with pleasure. When she bucked against him, he released a breath and joined her. His climax was almost violent, shaking his entire body. As he erupted inside her, he pressed his mouth to hers, both kissing and praising her at the same time. When he finally came back to earth, he looked down into her shining face. "Valerie..."

She shook her head, eyes squeezed shut. "I don't even know what to say."

He laughed softly and fell to her side to avoid crushing her. "That was fantastic." Pulling her closer, he sighed happily when she snuggled up next to him.

"I didn't know it could be like that," she murmured, rubbing her hands over his chest.

He frowned, "Like what?"

She hid her face against him before answering softly. "Slow and tender."

"How long were you married?" he asked curiously.

"Almost six years."

He wasn't sure how to respond. How could a man be married to this woman and not take the time to cherish her? Not once in six whole years?

Suddenly she wanted to curl into a ball and disappear. "I'm not complaining, George. My life with Craig was what it was."

He stroked her hair. "Okay."

"Really, I mean it."

"Val, you have nothing to prove to me," he assured her. "But slow and steady always wins the race."

She nipped at his shoulder and sighed. "I think I could get used to it."

Leaning over, he kissed her soundly. "I'll be right back." He disappeared briefly into the bathroom. When he returned, he slid under the covers and cuddled up to her. "I'd really like to sleep with you in my arms."

She gave him a surprised look, but curled a leg over his and sighed. Within minutes, she was breathing deeply.

He watched her for a few minutes, a feeling of possessiveness surging through him. It was more than sexual attraction that drew him to Val...she was a strong woman who knew her own mind. She was also great with Jess, which warmed his heart to no end. Stroking her arm, he closed his eyes and sighed. He could love this woman...

If there was any concern about how they would handle this new aspect of their relationship, it was reaffirmed in the early hours of the morning. George was more than happy to remind Val that slow and steady was definitely the way to reach their goal...twice.

By noon they knew they had to get up, but neither was ready to relinquish the closeness they had developed.

Rolling out of bed, George invited Val to join him in the tub. "It's big enough for two."

She smiled as she admired his naked body. She was not unaccustomed to a playful romp in the bathroom, but she was more used to inhabiting the shower stall. When he disappeared into the bathroom, she hopped up to follow him. He had already started the tub so she left briefly to retrieve her bubble bath.

He rolled his eyes but didn't make any comment when she dumped the floral scented concoction into his tub. Once the jets were going and the water level was good, he stepped in and sat at one end.

When he held out his hand for her, she stepped up and perched on the edge of the tub.

"C'mon in, the water is fine," he teased.

She carefully slipped into the tub facing him, then knelt between his legs. Instantly she was surrounded by bubbles and she braced her hands on his chest and kissed him. When his slick hands found her wet breasts, she moaned and pressed herself into his big palms. The moving water lapped around them while the jets pounded water against their legs.

He groaned and devoured her lips. The water made her body slippery and pliant under his fingers, which aroused him easily. Pulling back, he encouraged her to turn and sit with her back pressed against his chest. He wrapped his arms around her, holding her close to him. Burying his face in her hair, he inhaled the sweet scent of her mingled with the fragrant steam of the bath.

She tipped her head back into the hollow of his shoulder and smiled up at him. When he lowered his mouth to hers, she purred low in her throat.

He drew his hand up her chest to her throat, feeling her purr of contentment. His other hand dipped below the surface of the water to cup her mound. She sighed into his mouth when he began massaging her leisurely with a finger. When she relaxed her legs against his, opening herself wider to him, he dropped his hand from her throat to cup her breast.

She shuddered as he inserted two fingers inside her and stroked her slowly. Heat spiraled through her body, her toes curling in the still-warm water. As was his nature, he was slow and focused, reading her every response and responding in turn. She felt like she was drowning under his assaults on her so she dug her fingers into his thighs and hung on.

Reaching across to her other breast, he scraped the deserted nipple across the hair on his arm. He felt as well as heard her gasp in pleasure. Adjusting his other hand, he pressed his thumb against her nub and tweaked it. She groaned low in her throat and began undulating her hips against his hand. When she pulled away from his kiss, he focused his gaze on her. Her eyes were squeezed shut, her mouth was open and gasping for air. Lowering his eyes, he saw where his hand was fondling her breast and how her flesh was floating against the water. Bubbles caressed her, clinging to her free nipple and sliding along the slope of her breast. From there all he could see was his arm disappearing below the surface of the bubble-covered water. When he stroked her a little faster, she arched her head back against his shoulder and growled his name. He adjusted his hand again and pressed his two fingers in a forward position.

Val froze and stopped breathing. An intense pressure gripped her insides and tore a scream from her throat. She panted heavily and pressed her hips down on his fingers, holding him tightly inside her. It was almost impossible to stop moving against him and if he hadn't held onto her, she would have slipped beneath the surface of the water.

He held on tight, helping her ride wave after wave of her climax. When she finally went limp, he let go of a deep breath. He was hard as a rock beneath her, his body tight from participating in her arousal and climax. Reaching behind him, he grabbed a bottle of shampoo and squirted some into his hand. Then, with gentle strokes he began washing her hair.

She melted against him, letting her head fall forward so he could massage her scalp. "George...if you keep this up, I'm going to fall asleep right here."

"Tired?" he asked softly.

"Exhausted," she corrected. "And incredibly happy."

"Good." Cupping his hands, he rinsed the shampoo from her hair. "We should probably rinse off in the shower."

"And if I can't stand up?"

He grinned and kissed her neck. "I'll carry you." Leaning forward, he turned off the tub's jets. "Can you get up?"

"Ugh." She got to her feet slowly, then stepped out of the tub. Her legs wobbled slightly and she steadied herself with a hand on the wall. After a moment, she walked across the bathroom to the shower stall. As she was stepping in, George came up behind her.

"Looking a little unsteady on your feet there, darlin'," he teased, cupping her elbow to support her.

"Imagine that," she breathed, leaning against him as he turned on the warm water.

They took a leisurely shower, taking turns soaping each other up. Once they were clean, they scurried into the bedroom and into each others arms.

Val preceded George into his mother's kitchen. She was trying desperately to act normal but she felt as if she were glowing.

"Hi, Daddy!" Jess called, waving from the kitchen table where she and Maddie were coloring.

"Hi, sweets," he greeted his daughter. "Having fun with your cousin?"

"Sure," she chirped, giving Maddie the yellow crayon.

Val's gaze met Robyn's, then bounced away. "Did you leave us any food for dinner?"

"Of course not," Robyn interrupted, sliding out of her chair and grabbing Val's arm. "We should go talk about what we're going to eat." Without further conversation, she dragged Val from the room. She trundled up the stairs, pulling Val by the arm. Once they were behind closed doors, Robyn turned sharply. "Spill it."

Val opened her mouth to respond, but didn't get a chance.

"Don't even lie to me Valerie," Robyn warned her. "I'm pregnant and hormonal...no jury would convict me."

Sighing, Val plopped into a small arm chair. "George is going to know what we're talking about," she murmured.

"Who cares? Tell me, was it worth it?"

"No question," Val responded, clasping her hands together.

"Did you talk first?"

"Hardly," she laughed wryly. "He touched me and I was lost."

"What are you going to do now?" Robyn whispered.

Val shrugged and gazed across the room at her friend. "I have no clue." They both started when someone knocked on the bedroom door.

"Val? Robyn? Mom and Dad are back from the grocery store," Erik called through the closed door.

"We'll be right there," Robyn called back.

"You guys okay?"

"Of course," Robyn answered. "Just girl talk."

"Well can it and haul yourselves downstairs," he ordered sternly.

"It's a good thing there's a closed door between us, my love," Robyn sang sweetly.

"I'm no dummy," he called back before leaving them in silence.

"I guess we have to go downstairs," Val sighed. "And I have to keep my hands to myself."

"Just stay on the other side of the room," Robyn advised.

Val followed her back downstairs and into the kitchen. She greeted Ed and Marcy, then slid in to a chair next to Jess. Glancing up, she met George's gaze and gave him a small smile.

"Look at my picture," Jess demanded, tugging on Val's hand.

"It's lovely," Val told her, studying the picture of a house, tree and sun. In front of the house she had drawn some stick figure people and what looked like a horse. "Who is that?" she pointed to the horse.

"That's Spot the dog," Jess answered, giving her father a sly look. When he shook his head, she frowned and went back to her picture. "And that's me, and Daddy, and you."

Val's mouth fell open as Jess pointed out each of the stick figures and named them.

"Isn't that sweet," Marcy cooed, slicing leftover ham and placing it on a plate.

"Daddy, how old do I have to be to get a dog?" Jess asked casually, not looking up from her picture.

"Twenty-five," he answered just as casually.

She rolled her eyes and scooted closer to Val. "Don't you think I'm old enough to get a dog?"

Robyn hid a grin behind her hand and nudged her husband. This was how a child would play one parent against the other, as Maddie tried to do with them.

"I think a dog is a huge responsibility for anyone, let alone a child," Val answered carefully.

"I think a dog is a fine idea," Ed said jovially, smiling down at his eldest granddaughter.

"Then why don't you get one, Pop?" Erik asked.

"Because your mother won't let me," he complained.

"I'd be the one cleaning up after the mongrel," Marcy muttered under her breath.

"We can talk about a dog in a few years, sweets," George said, leaning against the counter. "When I think you're old enough to help care for it."

"But Val can help me take care of it," Jess pleaded.

"It's not nice of you to volunteer other people like that." George admonished her, not looking at Val, "This discussion is over."

Val stood. "Marcy, can I help you with anything?"

"No, hon, we have everything under control," Marcy said over her shoulder.

"Do you happen to have any fruit?" she asked.

"Sure," Marcy answered. "In the fridge."

"Do you mind if I throw together some dessert?"

"Go right ahead."

Val beckoned to Jess. "Go wash up so you can help me."

Jess hopped out of her chair and scurried off to the bathroom.

Heading for the fridge, she asked George to clean off a section of the table for her to work on. She opened the refrigerator and began gathering ingredients. Arms full, she returned to the table and set out the fruit.

"I'm all clean," Jess announced from Val's side. "What do we get to make?"

"Just hold your horses, missy," she tapped the end of Jess' nose. With permission from Marcy, she began rummaging in the kitchen pantry. "Perfect!" she crowed, holding up a box.

"Jell-O?" Erik made a face.

"You don't have to eat it," she said sweetly.

George watched her flit around, distracting Jess from the earlier dog conversation. She was gentle but firm with his daughter, letting her work alongside rather than taking over for her. Even with the help of a four year old, they were neat and efficient in creating a fun and tasty-looking parfait-like dessert. When Val laughed at something Erik said, his gut clenched with desire. She was beautiful, even with fruit and Jell-O smeared on her cheek. He was so busy watching her, he almost missed his mother watching him. She raised an eyebrow at him, but did not comment. He was sure she would catch up with him later.

He was right.

Chapter
Ten

Marcy held her son's arm as she shooed everyone out of the kitchen after dinner.

Trapped, he sighed and began rolling up his sleeves. He knew the routine...she would wash and ask questions, he would dry and answer them.

She waited until they were in a comfortable rhythm before speaking. "Things have changed?"

He blushed and concentrated on drying a dish. He was a grown man, married and a father...why was discussing his sex life so embarrassing? "Why would you say that?"

"Your smile is softer," she nudged his arm. "You are softer."

"It's not a big deal," he muttered.

"You are not the same man you were when you met Bernice. You have responsibilities, now," she reminded him. "Everything you do has repercussions."

"I know that."

"And Val is not Bernice," she warned. "She's already attached to your daughter and vice versa. Nothing about this is going to be simple."

"Nothing about Bernice was simple," he responded.

"Honey, in comparison to this, Bernice was a snap," her voice was sharp. "You didn't love Bernice...you barely knew her well enough to care about her. She was young, immature and totally uninterested in any kind of commitment. You could not have done anything to convince her to stay. With Val, she's firmly implanted in both yours and Jessica's life. She's a mature, loving and giving woman who cannot be easily brushed aside."

"I didn't brush Bernice aside."

"Oh yes, you did," she handed him another plate. "She may have made it easy for you, but you took what you wanted and just let her walk away."

He frowned at her interpretation of his relationship with his ex-wife.

"Can you imagine just letting Val walk away?" she asked softly. "And how that would affect Jess...she's not an unaware newborn now."

"But I would be dealing with these issues with any woman in my life," he protested.

"Not exactly. Val is in both of your lives twenty-four hours a day, seven days a week. This situation is nothing like Bernice," she stated firmly. "Just keep that in mind."

It was so easy for Val to settle into this relationship with George. They were careful around Jess, keeping their touches light and casual, but in private they were comfortably affectionate. It was like they were any other family, living quietly within their neighborhood, supporting each other on a daily basis.

She was happy caring for Jess and George, keeping house and silently loving both of them. It was no surprise to her that life with George was gentle and tender, fulfilling her in a way Craig never had. They spent most evenings at home, content to be in each other's company...reading, watching a movie or spending time with Jess. When they went out, it was as a threesome and they all enjoyed it.

Christmas was just around the corner when she got the surprise of a lifetime. She was in the kitchen, baking cookies for Jess' class party when the doorbell rang. Since it was Monday and Jess was still in class, she had to scurry down the hall to answer the door. Without looking through the peephole, she threw open the door. Staring at the man on the doorstep, her jaw slack, she stood frozen.

"Hello, Val."

With a jerk, she snapped her mouth shut and straightened her spine. "What are you doing here, Craig?"

He frowned and rocked back on his heels. "I've been looking for you."

"Why?"

"I've missed you, Val. I think I made a mistake when I let you go," he responded.

"You left me, Craig...," she whispered. "Why in heaven's name would you be looking for me?"

"Listen, lets go out to dinner and talk about this..."

"How did you find me?" she interrupted.

"I finally persuaded your lawyer to tell me." He took a step forward and reached for her cheek. "I told her what a huge mistake I'd made and that I wanted to beg for your forgiveness." What he'd really done was hire a private eye to find out where she'd disappeared to.

She glared at his outstretched hand until he dropped it to his side. "Go home, Craig. I'm not interested in anything else you have to say."

"Val," he pleaded. "Can't we try again? We were good together...we had fun together. What kind of fun can you be having out here in nowhere, Pennsylvania, keeping house for some stranger?"

"Go home, Craig."

"Until we talk, my home is here. I'm staying at the Days Inn, room three twelve." This time he did touch her cheek. "I'm not going back to Maryland without you. We belong together, Val, and you know it."

She stepped back and closed the door firmly. He was as handsome as she remembered, but there was something new in his tanned face. He was still blond haired, blue eyed, boy-next-door good looking, but that was where it ended. She knew where her initial attraction had come from, but why had she stayed with him so long?

Pushing away from the door, she suddenly realized that the air was thick with the smell of burnt cookies. "Oh damn!" Running down the hall, she cursed long and loud, calling Craig every name in the book. If he could even fathom that she would go back to him, then he really had lost his marbles. She pulled the burnt cookies from the oven and dropped the pan onto the stove top. She would have to air out the smoky oven before putting in the next batch.

She was still cursing under her breath when she left to pick up

Jess. Once they were home again, she let Jess help her decorate the cookies that were already finished. While Jess was busy at the kitchen table, she stood at the counter, cursing silently and remixing batter to replace the ruined cookies.

George parked the car in the one-car garage and got out. As he was pulling the door shut, a florist's van pulled up in front of the house. He stood silently, expecting the guy to check his clipboard and drive away. When he exited the van and opened the rear door, George frowned. Who would be sending him flowers? The floral arrangement that appeared from inside the truck was extravagant and obviously expensive. Shifting from one foot to another, he waited for the delivery guy to approach him.

Val heard the front door open, then close. With a smile, she waited for George to appear in the kitchen doorway. When he did, her smile broadened.

"Daddy!" Jess squealed. "What pretty flowers!"

He greeted his daughter, then carried the flowers to the counter. "They're for Val."

Her smile softened as she looked down at the beautiful bouquet. "Oh, George...what a wonderful surprise. You're so sweet! Thank you."

Clearing his throat, he finally met her gaze. "Don't thank me."

Her smile faded, then disappeared. "What do you mean?"

"I ran into the delivery man outside," he responded. "I had nothing to do with this."

"Then who...?" When he shrugged, she closed her eyes and swallowed. "Oh, no." Her hand shaking, she reached for the card nestled into the greenery. Knowing even before she opened the card, she peeled away the envelop and stared at the small piece of paper.

"Who gave you them?" Jess piped up in the silence.

"An...an old friend," she responded hesitantly. Without any further comment, she dropped the card and envelop into the trash.

"What do you want me to do with them?"

She turned back to her cookie sheet and shrugged. "Why don't you put them into the other room. Or maybe put them in the front hall." *Anywhere...just get them away from me,* she thought wildly. Glancing into the trash can, he could only see the signature on the card. It very neatly said "Craig". What the hell was going on? Why was she getting flowers from her ex-husband? They had not really discussed their new relationship but he was pretty sure that they shouldn't be seeing other people. With one last look at the side of her face, he turned and left the room.

She watched him go, then closed her eyes. What was wrong with Craig? She had practically slammed the door in his face and he sent flowers. And just like Craig, the bouquet was wildly flamboyant and outrageous.

"Val?"

She opened her eyes and focused her gaze on Jess' worried face. "Yes, honey?"

"Are you okay? You have a funny look on your face," Jess whispered. "Like you're going to throw up."

Val groaned softly, trying to rearrange her features into a neutral mask. "I'm fine, sweets. I think I've just been standing near the hot oven too long."

"Oh," Jess sprinkled some green candies onto a cookie. "Then why did Daddy have the same look?"

Sighing, Val tried to concentrate on the cookies. "I don't know. Maybe he had a bad day."

Jess cocked her head and watched Val for a moment. "Why did your friend send you flowers?"

"Because he missed me, I guess."

"Oh! Can we send flowers to Jennifer?" Jess asked, distracted by this new thought.

"Lets ask your Dad first, okay?"

"'Kay," she chirped, returning to the cookies laid out in front of her.

As he was cleaning up after dinner, George noted that the flowers had disappeared from the kitchen. When Val went out for her walk, he followed Jess upstairs to give her a bath. As he waited for Jess to gather her pajamas, he poked his head into Val's bedroom, but the flowers were not there, either.

Later that evening, he found them when he was taking out the trash. They were stuffed haphazardly into the plastic garbage can. He stood there for a moment, staring at the crushed flowers in confusion. What did all of this mean? Was she an unwilling recipient? Why was her ex back in her life? And what did he want?

Val was hoping that if she ignored the card and flowers, then Craig would go away. No such luck. He showed up on her doorstep again on Wednesday, just before lunch time.

Opening the front door, she sighed loudly and did not greet him.

Craig refused to flinch under her hard gaze. "Hi, Val."

"Now what?"

He shifted from one foot to another. "Did I tell you how beautiful you are?"

She placed her hands on her hips and glared at him. "How could you ignore the fact that I told you I'm not interested?"

"I know you're mad at me, Val," he said in his most contrite voice. "But I'm telling you that I was wrong...we should never have split up."

"I am not interested in a reconciliation."

"Can I come in?" he pleaded.

"No," she said sharply, standing in the center of the doorway to block his entrance.

"Then let me take you to lunch," he offered. "We belong together, you and me. You don't need to be here...you're better than this job...this two-bit town! Come home with me and let me take care of you."

"You're going to take care of me just like you used to? No, thank you," she said scathingly. "I barely got out from under your 'care', and I have no urge to return."

"Okay," he said soothingly, holding out his hands. "I didn't do so great a job, but I will now. You mean everything to me, Val. I'm nothing without you." Pausing, he lowered his voice. "I miss you, baby. I miss your lush body next to mine at night. I miss making love to you...waking up next to you. Remember how good we were together? How exciting sex was for us? We never could get enough of each other." His eyes gleamed as he eyed her up and down. "We worked every room of the house, didn't we?"

She flushed and looked around the quiet street. "Sex isn't everything, Craig. What I needed from you was trust."

"I trust you, baby," he murmured absently, touching her arm.

"But I can't trust you." She took one step back so that his hand fell away from her body. "I'm going to be very clear, Craig. I don't want you here. I'm not coming back to you. Go home!"

He frowned and tried to peer around her into the house. "Are you sleeping with the boss, Val? Is that why you're refusing to come home to your husband?"

"You are my ex-husband and that means my life is no business of yours. I suggest you leave now before you say something you'll really regret."

"Is it the house? Because I can get you a house bigger and better than this one." When she glared at him in silence, he continued agreeably. "Okay, I'll leave, for the time being. But I'm not giving up on you or on us." Turning away, he strode confidently to a dark blue car parked at the curb.

She didn't even wait for him to get in his car and drive off, instead she slammed the front door loudly and stomped away.

Val sat alone in the family room, the TV showing some old black and white movie. She was so engrossed in her own thoughts that she didn't see George enter.

"Hey," he settled onto the couch next to her.

"Hi." She scooted closer and snuggled into his side. "Jess all clean and tucked in?"

"Yup." Wrapping an arm around her shoulders, he sighed tiredly. "She's so excited about Christmas. Do you mind that we're spending Christmas Day with my parents?"

"Of course not. I like your mom and dad."

"Well, I wondered if you wanted to spend Christmas with Robyn and Erik," he murmured, rubbing her shoulder with his big hand.

"No, they're spending Christmas with Robyn's parents," she told him, letting her head drop back onto his arm. She closed her eyes and rolled her face toward him. It was only a moment later when she felt his warm lips on hers.

"Val?"

She loved this quiet time together with him. "Hmm?"

"I need to ask you...," he paused and lifted his head. "I need to ask you about the flowers."

Her eyes flew open and a wry smile spread across her face. "What?"

"I thought you would be too polite to ask," she answered softly. "The flowers were from Craig."

"Why?"

"He has the foolish notion that he wants to get back together," was her honest answer.

"Did he call you?"

"He stopped by," she paused. "Twice."

He frowned and pulled away from her. "Why didn't you tell me?"

"I wanted to handle it. He's my ex, my problem."

"So is he going away now?"

Sighing, she got to her feet and paced in front of the coffee table. "I told him to go home. I told him that there was no chance of us getting back together."

"But he doesn't agree," he crossed one leg over the other. "I can't really blame him."

She stopped and stared at him. "What?"

"I certainly don't want to let you go. Why would he?"

"George..."

"Seriously, Val, I understand where he's coming from. But even so, I'm not going to let him continue to harass you." He stood and went to grasp her by the shoulders. "Where is he?"

"He's staying in a local motel." She looked up into his handsome face, "But I really think he'll just get bored and go home. Please, don't be upset, just let it go."

"I don't want him bothering you."

"I was pretty blunt with him today. I don't think he'll be back." Caressing his cheek, she smiled teasingly. "Lets just forget about him and go upstairs, okay?"

He swept his hands along her shoulders and up to frame her face. "Upstairs? Who wants to wait that long?"

Later, George lay in the darkness of his bedroom, Val cuddled at his side. He was angry. He was angry at Craig for bothering Val and interrupting his blissful world. He was also angry at Val for not telling him what was going on. It was his job to take care of her, look out for her, protect her. How was he supposed to do any of that if she didn't tell him what was going on?

He looked over at her, his gaze caressing her beautiful face. In her sleep, she looked peaceful and content. He would not allow Craig to take her happiness away. Brushing a finger over her soft, smooth cheek, he silently promised her that he would get rid of the vermin trying to invade her life.

Chapter
Eleven

On Friday, both George and Jess stayed home to pick out a tree and begin decorating the house for Christmas. Once they had dragged the tree into the house and set it on the stand, George disappeared to retrieve decorations from the attic.

In the family room, Val was teaching Jess how to string popcorn. They were having more fun trying to throw the big kernels into each other's mouths.

"Hey there!" George called from the archway. "Stop that!"

Jess giggled up at her father. "I got ten into Val's mouth."

"And about a jillion onto the floor," he complained, setting two big boxes onto the floor.

Rolling her eyes, Jess scrambled across the floor to peek into the boxes. She sat next to George, patiently helping him unwrap ornaments for the tree. When she found one particular ornament, she cradled it carefully and crossed to share it with Val.

"What do you have there?" Val asked, still working on the popcorn.

"This is my ornament," she whispered, holding out her hand.

Val looked at the tiny baby ornament in her little hand. The baby was blond, swaddled in a pink blanket and laying in a beautiful yellow bassinet. The bassinet was sitting on top of the year that Jess was born. "That's lovely, Jess."

"We got this when I was born."

"Did Daddy buy that for you?" She looked over at George but he had a peculiar look on his face.

"No. Mommy bought it for me before she left." She stood and skipped over to the tree to hang the ornament.

Val was shocked at the little girl's blunt statement. When she looked over at George, he had a similar look on his face.

"Where did you hear that, sweets?" he gasped.

"I don't know," she shrugged and returned to continue unpacking ornaments.

He stood and started unwinding some lights for the tree. He had absolutely no idea what to say.

"What else do you know about your mommy?" Val asked casually, her gaze again focused on her string of popcorn.

"I look like her."

"I remember your Uncle Erik saying that at Thanksgiving." Val continued, trying to stay calm, "She must have been very beautiful."

Jess started hanging more ornaments on the tree. She made no more comments about her absentee parent.

They worked in silence for a few minutes until the doorbell rang. George hopped up to answer it. He threw open the front door, the cold air hitting his face, and stared at the man on the other side.

"Hi. Is Val around?"

George frowned at the cheerful greeting. "Who are you?"

"I'm Craig," he held out his hand to shake.

"What do you want?" George knew he was being rude, but he didn't care.

"I was looking for Val," Craig repeated. "Is she home?"

"I don't think she's interested in seeing you." He started when Val appeared at his side.

"What's going on here?" she asked sharply.

"I stopped by to see you, Val," Craig said smoothly, his gaze raking her voluptuous figure. She was wearing a green sweater that hugged her rounded body and darkened her eyes to a moss green.

"I told you not to come back, Craig." She stepped in front of George and glared at the man on the front stoop.

"I knew you didn't mean it. Lets go talk alone...there's plenty of privacy in my hotel room," he offered.

"Daddy," Jess appeared silently. "Who's that man?"

Craig's eyes narrowed as his gaze bounced from Jess back to Val. "I'm a friend of Valerie's."

Jess brightened. "Did you send those pretty flowers?"

"I sure did, kiddo," he smiled at her. "But they weren't half as pretty as you."

George growled low in his throat and placed his hands on his daughter's tiny shoulders.

Val threw George a look. "Why don't you and Jess go into the kitchen, get warm and have some cookies while I say goodbye to our guest."

"Can he have some cookies, too?" Jess asked.

"Craig doesn't want any cookies," Val told her, pushing her gently toward the kitchen. "Go on, I'll join you in a minute."

George left them, but only after one final glare at Craig.

"It's the kid, isn't it?" Craig queried, stepping closer.

"What about her?" she asked, wrapping her arms around herself to keep warm.

"We could have our own, you know. You wouldn't have to raise someone else's kid."

"What makes you think I'd want to have a child with you? I can't believe one word out of your mouth! I would never subject a child to that," she hissed. She had lived that way as a child and would not allow her blood to suffer like that.

"What are you talking about? I did everything I could to take care of you."

"No," she interrupted. "You *said* you were taking care of me when instead you were quietly running up our debt and ruining my credit."

"You have to spend money to make money, Val."

She started when George reappeared and silently nudged her aside.

"Let me see you to your car, Adamson," he addressed Craig.

"George...," Val began.

"Jess is waiting for you in the kitchen," he told her, stepping out onto the stoop and straightening to his full height. Even through his sweater he could feel the cold air pressing at him.

She frowned and turned on her heel. Maybe George could talk some sense into Craig.

George closed the door behind him, then crossed his arms over

RIDA ALLEN

his chest. "You're done here and I don't expect you to return."

"This is none of your business," Craig said mildly.

"Val is in my employ and it is my duty to make sure she is safe in my home. If you set foot on my property again, I'll contact the police," George responded.

Craig eyed him. "She's more than just an employee, isn't she?"

George remained silent, his face an impassive mask.

"Did she tell you what a great sex life we had? We used to do it everywhere...in every position you can imagine," Craig taunted. "Val's not a small woman, but she certainly is flexible. And she was more than willing to enjoy new places and positions with me. You can't say that, can you? But you know what?" he continued thoughtfully. "She'll probably be loyal to you, no matter how boring the sex is. Because she's one of those women who value hearth and home over personal happiness. Despite all my "budget" problems, she stayed with me. If I hadn't walked away from her, we'd still be together because that's the kind of gal she is." He paused to study George briefly, "So it's no wonder you'd want her for more than just a housekeeper."

George just glared at the shorter man, making no comment.

"Well," Craig said cheerfully, stepping back. "I'm not going to promise to give up."

"Don't come back on my property, don't call my house, do not contact Val," George said firmly. "You might as well just go back to your little, desperate life and try to find some other woman to con."

"We'll see," Craig practically sang as he turned and trotted to his car. "Nice chatting with you, Greg."

George didn't bother to correct him, just stood silently in the cold until Craig drove away. On the outside, he was a stoic soldier...on the inside he was churning with thoughts and doubts. Some of the things Craig had said hit a nerve. He was a down-to-earth guy and preferred to keep all parts of his life on a simple, even keel. At least, as much as was possible with a four year old daughter. He enjoyed a quiet night at home and tender, gentle moments with his lover. Did Val miss the excitement that had apparently been a part of her sex life prior? Would she plant herself in a relationship so securely that nothing, not even her own unhappiness, could uproot her? Is that what she was doing with him?

Kicking a rock off the sidewalk, he turned and re-entered the house. He found Val and Jess back in the family room, unwrapping ornaments and laying them out on the couch and coffee table.

Val looked up at his entrance. "Everything all right?"

His eyes swept her beautiful face, coming to rest on her sweet lips. Was she lying to him about her happiness? Was she breaking her own rule of telling only the truth? "Yeah, he's gone."

"He was always persistent," she murmured, watching his facial expressions. "It's what made him good at his job. So, did he say anything else?"

Shrugging, he crossed the room to pick up the lights. "Why don't you help me wrap these around the tree."

She stood and joined him next to the fragrant spruce. "Did he say something to upset you?"

"Other than the fact that he's not going to give up?" he asked sarcastically.

Frowning, she stepped back from the tree without taking the light strand he was holding out to her. "Jess, why don't you come help your Daddy with these lights? I'm going to make us all some hot chocolate." With that, she turned stiffly and left the room.

He watched her go, wanting to follow her and apologize for snapping at her, but he didn't. He was angry that he let Craig's comments get to him, but they swirled around in his head nonetheless.

To Val's relief, Craig did not reappear over the weekend. However, her relationship with George seemed to have shifted almost imperceptibly. She was making a pumpkin pie Monday evening when he wandered into the kitchen and sat down at the table.

"Where did you learn to cook?" he asked softly.

She looked up from her task, her eyes caressing his handsome features. She could stare at him for hours and never tire. "When I was in foster care. Often it was the woman who was at home during the day to care for the kids...and we were usually given chores. My favorite was always to help the foster mom prepare meals. When I was a teenager, I stayed with a family where the man did a lot of the cooking...I learned a lot about down-home cooking from him."

He listened to her voice as she spoke about her childhood. There was a warmth, a fondness he would not have expected from someone who had grown up with strangers.

"It seems like each home I went to, I learned something new. Cookies here, pies there, cakes the next place...and always good, solid foods," she continued. "When I moved out on my own, I was comfortable enough with my cooking skills to start experimenting on my own. I enjoy it...it reminds me of fun times and allows me to be creative."

"Did you ever think of becoming a chef?"

Finishing off the pie, she covered it and put it away for the time being. She poured herself a cup of coffee and joined him at the table. "I have in the past." Taking a sip of the hot drink, she paused to gather her words, "I enjoy cooking and would be concerned that doing it every day as a trade would make it a 'job'. It would no longer be fun, it would be work."

"You don't think it's possible to do what you enjoy?"

"I enjoy cooking for my friends. That's enough for me," she said firmly.

He reached out and touched her soft cheek. How could any man walk away from this precious woman? Craig had been right, she truly was the epitome of hearth and home. "Why didn't you have children while you were married?"

"Deep down, I wasn't sure that Craig and I were ready," she answered thoughtfully. "We would spend a lot of evenings entertaining his clients or going out for fun. I didn't think that was the right time to raise a child."

"Are you sorry that you made that decision?"

Frowning, she studied his face. "I don't think there's any good way to answer that. I can only be content with what I have right now."

"I guess I can understand that."

"What about you? Do you have regrets about how you got to where you are now?" she wanted to know.

"I never wanted to hurt Bernice. And I can honestly say that I did not get involved with her with the thought of having a child." He was trying to be brutally honest. "But when it happened, I felt like it happened for a reason. And I could not turn away from it."

"What did Bernice want?" she whispered hesitantly.

"I thought she wanted to have the baby," he said quietly, aware that his daughter was just upstairs. "But we really didn't discuss it very much once the decision was made. I thought if I offered to take care of her every need that would be enough for her."

"Did you love her?"

"I don't think so but I did enjoy the idea of becoming a family. Up until that point, I'd been the playboy, the gigolo. And I enjoyed the hell out of it...for a while." Reaching out, he snagged her cup and took a drink of the lukewarm brew. "After a while, I realized how unhappy I was flitting from one woman to another. So when Bernice got pregnant, I took it as a sign."

"Where did you meet her?"

"At a restaurant. She was our waitress," he thought back to that night. He and his friends had stopped by a chain restaurant for a bite on their way to a basketball game. When Bernice had come to take their order, he had been immediately captivated by her laugh and her outgoing attitude. Before leaving he had traded some casual flirtations with her, along with phone numbers. "She was tall, blond and so vivacious...and she seemed so happy. Who wouldn't want to be with someone like that?"

She frowned, thinking that she was totally opposite of what he had just described as his ideal woman. So why would he want to be with her? "What happened?"

"I'm not sure. After she got pregnant and we got married, we didn't talk. I mean, we spoke to each other, but we never really discussed anything important." He shrugged, "I guess I never asked her if she was happy because I never wanted to know. Ignorance is bliss, right?"

"How long did she stick around?"

"We stayed married for a couple of weeks after Jess was born, but she wasn't really here. She went home to her parents in Texas only two weeks after delivery. When she came back, it was to ask for a divorce." Rubbing his forehead, he tried to remember that conversation. He struggled to recall if he had even been surprised...or if he had even asked Bernice to stay.

"I'm sorry, George," Val said quietly, watching him deal with some strong emotion.

He looked up at her, wondering if they too were avoiding important conversations. Was she happy in their relationship? Was there something he could be doing to make her happier? Her green eyes were warm with sympathy, her body tilted toward him in compassion. Letting his gaze roam over her full breasts, he felt a surge of desire for her. Could he go to her and take her passionately here in the kitchen?

Even as a young bachelor, he had always held tight control over his body and his passion. He had been a playboy around his friends, flirting outrageously and often. But once he had gotten the woman alone, he had always been tender in his passion. He had never taken a woman without regards to her fulfillment. Not once had he found hasty pleasure in the backseat of a car or locked in a public restroom. Yes, he and Val had made love in the family room, on the couch, but he had been his regular gentle self. Did Val crave more? He sat silently as she touched his hand, then rose to place her coffee cup in the sink.

Shoving back his chair with such force that it toppled backwards, he strode across the room and caught her against the counter.

She gasped as he pressed against her and lowered his mouth to hers. His body was hot and hard under her hands and she groaned at the feel of him.

He placed his hands at her waist and lifted her up to sit on the counter. Pushing her legs apart, he settled himself against her and gripped the back of her head. He devoured her lips and surged against her when she wrapped her legs around his waist. Panting, he pulled away from her mouth, grasped the front of her blouse and ripped it open.

Moaning, she gripped his arms, her fingers digging into his flesh. As the buttons from her shirt flew off and landed haphazardly around the room, he blinked. He could hear each button impact and come to rest. What was he doing? Chest heaving, he groaned and unclasped Val's legs to step away from her. Silently he found and retrieved each of her buttons, then laid them in her hand. "I can't do this." With that final anguished statement, he turned and left the room.

She watched him go, mouth agape her outstretched palm cradling five small, white buttons. Had he been so lost in his memories of Bernice that he'd gotten caught up in the moment and begun ravishing her? Had he come to his senses, realized that it was her he was touching and been disappointed? Sliding off the counter to the floor, she righted the kitchen chair, then tiptoed through the house and up the stairs. Once inside her bedroom, she stripped off her shirt and tossed it and the buttons into the trash. She could have fixed it...sewing five buttons onto a shirt was simple...but she knew she would not wear that blouse again.

George sat in the darkness of his bedroom, feet planted flat on the floor, head cradled in his hands. Oh how he'd wanted Val...just the thought of being buried inside her made his gut ache with desire. But to take her like an animal, to maul that beautiful body that deserved to be worshiped...he couldn't do it. What must Val be thinking? He wanted to go to her, to explain what had happened, but he was afraid. If they started this discussion, there was no telling where it would end and he wasn't sure he was ready for that.

Flopping backward onto the bed, he groaned and stared at the ceiling. Since Thanksgiving they had spent every night together, wrapped in each others arms. He doubted that she would come to him tonight and he was far too embarrassed to go to her. How could he possibly explain himself? *I was trying to be the man you want and just couldn't do it?* Knowing Val, she would tell him he was being silly and that he was exactly what she wanted...but would it be the truth? She demanded the truth from him, but would she be able to face up to him with her truths?

The questions just whipped around inside his head, making him dizzy and tired. Without bothering to get undressed, he flung his legs up on the bed and closed his eyes.

Chapter
Twelve

The next morning, Val couldn't even look George in the eyes. She was humiliated by last night's episode in the kitchen and could only assume that he felt the same. Memories of his ex-wife setting off his desires was not something she wanted to discuss with him.

After dropping Jess off at preschool, Val headed for the nearest shopping mall. She had already bought a few Christmas gifts for both Jess and Ed, but still needed to find something for Marcy and George. She was unsure what to get Marcy and now even more concerned about a gift for George.

In the mall's major department store, she found a beautiful blouse for Marcy. In addition, she found a long gold necklace with a large heart pendant on it to go with the cream-colored blouse. Clutching her bag of purchases, she wandered out into the mall. There were stores of every kind around her, but she had no idea where to even begin. As she window shopped, she found a stuffed animal that she couldn't resist buying for Jess.

Peering into a men's store, she suddenly realized from the reflective glass that someone was staring at her. She turned around and spotted Craig lounging against a banister.

"Hiya, Val," he called out, pushing away from the railing to join her.

"Are you following me?" she asked incredulously.

"I don't know what you're talking about. This is a public place and I just happened to be here at the same time as you," he answered innocently.

She turned on her heel and stalked off.

"Hey!" he grabbed her arm. "Where are you going?"

"You weren't here to see me, remember? So let me go so we can both go about our business," she hissed, wrenching her arm from his grasp.

He fell into step next to her. "It's a happy accident that I ran into you," his voice was cheerful. "Why shouldn't I take advantage of it?"

She tried to ignore him, keeping her head turned away as if she were inspecting each store's window display.

"Shopping for anything good today?" he tried to peer into her bag.

"Quit that!" she snatched the bag away from him.

"Val, Val...," he admonished. "Don't be so mean to me. I love you. I want you." Looking around, he pointed to a sign on their left, "C'mon, lets sneak in there and make out."

She barely glanced at the restroom sign and continued walking. "Go away. I don't want to be with you in any way."

He grabbed her arm again, stopping her in her tracks. "Listen to me!" he demanded. "I'm done playing games with you. I want you to come home with me right now. You can leave your things and we'll send for them later."

She drew up to her full height, a scant four inches shorter than him, and glared at his angry face. "I am not your possession...you do not own me. If you do not release me right now, I will scream bloody murder and draw every security guard and cop within a two mile radius," her voice brooked no argument. "I mean it, Craig. We are never going to be together again."

"Val..."

Frowning at the pleading tone in his voice, she withdrew her arm from his hand. "If you come near me again, Craig, I will get a restraining order. Don't let the good memories of our marriage disintegrate any more than they already have. Move on with your life like I have with mine."

He snarled at her. "You'll never be happy with that boring housefrau of a man."

"My life is my own to live as I see fit. Good-bye, Craig." Before he could respond, she strode off at high-speed. She was almost afraid to look over her shoulder to see if he had followed her. When she finally did, she was relieved that there seemed to be no sign of him. Checking her watch, she groaned. She only had a short window of time to finish her shopping before she had to leave to pick up Jess from school.

Val sat quietly in her bedroom wrapping all her gifts. For safety's sake, she had wrapped Jess' gifts during the day while she was busy at preschool. Tomorrow, while George was at work, she would help Jess wrap her gifts for him and for his parents.

Outside her closed door, she heard George and Jess laughing as they moved from bath-time to bedtime. Soon Jess would be tucked in for the night and George would retire to the family room to watch television. She could almost guarantee that he would not turn-in before midnight since this had become his pattern for the past few nights. For her part, she was in bed with the lights out by ten, just in case he came upstairs early.

Placing her last piece of scotch tape, she set the colorfully wrapped package aside. She stood and stretched, her back aching with stress and fatigue. There were bonuses to having large breasts, but there were also drawbacks. One of them was dealing with an aching back and shoulders at the end of a long day.

Quickly she changed into her robe and cracked open her bedroom door. The hallway was empty so she scurried into the bathroom she shared with Jess. She turned on the shower, shed her robe and stepped under the warm spray.

George let his head fall back against the recliner. He could hear the shower running upstairs and an image of Val popped into his head. She was standing in his shower stall, her wet hair plastered to her head, her full mouth smiling up at him. He missed her...everything about her. They were living in the same house but it was like they were strangers again. He couldn't even get her to look him in the face, how was he going to explain what had happened to him that night in the kitchen?

Christmas was fast approaching and he could not imagine going through the holidays without holding Val in his arms. He loved the holidays...the fun and enjoyment of watching his daughter and parents open their gifts. And this year, he would be able to see Val, too. But would she glow with joy or continue to stay far away from him?

He jumped in his chair when the phone rang. Picking up the receiver off the table, he spoke into the phone. "Hello?"

"George?"

He couldn't place the voice. "Yes?"

"It's Bernie."

His mouth dropped open in surprise. "Is this a joke?" He flinched when she laughed in his ear.

"No, it's no joke. It's me."

"Well, I must say that this is unexpected," he said quietly. "May I ask why you're calling?"

"I know I gave up all my rights..."

"Yes, you did," he interrupted. "And it's all very legal, as you well remember."

"I know that," she responded. "I just wondered...how is she?"

He frowned at the strange tone in her voice. "She's fine. Healthy and quite happy."

"I think about her, George, all the time."

"You made your decision a long time ago, Bernie."

"I know," she whispered almost brokenly. "I just wasn't ready."

"There's no need to rehash any of this. All the decisions that needed to be made are finished. We really have nothing more to discuss about Jessica," he said flatly.

"Jessica...," her voice was tentative as she murmured the name.

Clutching the phone in a death-grip, he fumed over the thought that she hadn't even remembered Jess' name.

"George...could you...would you send me a picture? Just one...," she asked.

"Why? You weren't interested then, why should you get to reap any rewards from Jess' life?" he exploded.

She gasped and choked down a sob. "People change, George. There's a hole..."

"You created the hole, Bernie. Live with that."

"I don't want her to think she wasn't wanted..."

"Don't you worry, kid, Jess knows very well how much I love her. Her grandparents dote on her as does Val...," he snapped his mouth shut.

"Val? Did you remarry, George?"

He heard the slurred quality of her voice, as if she were crying.

"My life is my business. Be assured that Jess is in good hands and will never want for anything, including love."

"Please, George, just one picture," she begged.

"I'm not going to get involved in this Bernie. If you have any questions about our legal agreement, you can contact my lawyer," he said angrily.

"I'm sorry, George," she sobbed into the phone. "Please don't shut me out of her life..."

"Good bye, Bernie," he said softly before disconnecting.

Val froze at the top of the stairs as George's hushed good bye floated up to her. Oh, the way he whispered her name...it was so much worse than she had imagined! She barely swallowed a groan before whirling away from the steps. That was it, she couldn't stay a moment longer.

Back in her room, the door shut firmly, she picked up the phone and called her best friend.

"Calm down," Robyn told her. "You have to be mistaken...Bernice is way out of the picture."

"Not anymore. I heard him, Robyn. Please, can I crash with you for a while?"

"You know you're always welcome here, Val. But lets just talk this through for a minute," Robyn's voice was firm and reassuring. "You cannot leave Jess like this...just disappear like her mother did. You need to be rational."

"God, Robyn, what did I get myself into?"

"Maybe it's a good time for you to find an apartment of your own. You could continue to care for Jess, but not be stuck in that house with George 24/7," she suggested.

"I have got to get out of here," Val whispered. "How can I face him, knowing that I wasn't a good enough substitute for his ex-wife?"

"I am so sure you're wrong about this, Val," Robyn muttered crossly. "Give me thirty minutes and I'll call you back."

"Robyn, no!" But her best friend had already hung up on her. Dropping the dead receiver into its cradle, she buried her head in her hands. As far as she knew, George hadn't been in touch with Bernice since she walked away from her new family. But here, after having spent time with Val, he found her so lacking in comparison that he contacted Bernice. What was she going to do? She could not sit here and watch as he attempted to woo Bernice back into his life.

When the phone rang a few minutes later, she snatched up the receiver after only one ring. "Hello?"

"Look," Robyn began without any greeting. "He is not getting back with Bernice."

"It doesn't matter. I can't stay here knowing that it's her he longs for," Val whispered.

"Christmas is just a few days away. Hang tough until then and we'll be up the next week. And if you really want, you can come home with us after New Year's," Robyn promised.

"New Year's...," she shuddered and closed her eyes. "I don't know if I can stand it that long."

"You can do it. Be strong and concentrate on taking care of that precious little girl."

"Right...concentrate on Jess."

"Get some rest and we'll see you after Christmas."

"Sure...okay." After muttering a good bye, she hung up the phone. Christmas eve was only two days away...she could stick it out, be an adult. And when Robyn and Erik arrived, she would tell George of her impending departure.

It was just as difficult as she had expected. George kept watching her and she tried desperately not to be left alone with him.

Christmas eve, after dinner, the three of them spent the evening in the family room, watching one of Jess' favorite Disney movies.

George sat in his recliner and Jess curled up with Val on the couch. The two girls were loudly crunching on popcorn as cartoon characters sang and danced on the TV.

"Val," Jess whispered. "I want to be like Belle."

"Oh yeah?" Val whispered back. "You want to live in France and sing to your chickens?"

"No! I want to be beautiful and live with my daddy."

Val closed her eyes and hugged the little girl. "You already have those things, sweetie."

"I want to be all growed up and be beautiful and live with my daddy," Jess corrected herself.

"It's no picnic to be grown up, Jess. Take your time, okay?"

Jess didn't respond, just cuddled against Val and focused on the TV.

Behind her, Val could feel George staring at her again. Frowning, she scrunched lower on the couch and fixed her eyes on the TV.

An hour later, Jess was sound asleep and the movie was over.

"Don't move," George ordered as he turned off the TV and VCR. "I'll take her up and put her to bed." He leaned over to scoop Jess into his arms and accidentally brushed across Val's breast. When she gasped and sank away from him, he cursed. Lifting his daughter into his arms, he spat, "Do not move...we are going to talk."

She frowned and opened her mouth to argue, but changed her mind at his glare. "Fine."

He turned on his heel and left the room, Jess clutched against his chest.

Val sat in the darkened room, the only light coming from the decorations on the Christmas tree. She was not looking forward to this conversation...there was no way it could turn out well. If she had any place to go, she would be running for the door right now. After a few minutes of tomb-like silence, George reappeared in the archway.

"Val..."

"You don't need to explain anything to me," she blurted nervously.

He stopped in his tracks and stared at her through the darkness. "What?"

She pulled her knees up toward her chest and wrapped her arms around her legs. "You don't owe me anything. What you do is your business."

After a moment of silence, he stepped farther into the room and perched on the edge of the recliner seat. "What exactly do you think I've been doing?"

"It's not important," she murmured, loathe to even speak the woman's name. "I'm just saying that you don't have to answer to me."

"I think I'm missing something here."

She uncurled herself and stood, edging her way toward the hall. "It's fine, no big deal. But I might as well tell you now that I'm going back to Maryland after New Year's."

His jaw dropped. "What! Why?"

"I just think it's for the best," she said softly.

"Val, I'm completely confused," he stood and followed her into the hallway. "Why would you leave us? We need you."

Tears pressed against the back of her eyes. "Please don't make this any harder than it already is."

"Don't walk away from me, Val. Tell me what the hell is going on," he demanded, grabbing her arm.

She swallowed carefully past the lump in her throat. "You should start looking for someone else to care for Jess. I'm sure it won't be difficult for you." With that, she gently extricated her arm and hurried up the stairs to her room.

George stood at the base of the steps, his heart pounding in his chest. How could she just leave them like this? She wasn't even giving him a chance to fix what had gone wrong. He wanted to storm up there and demand that she listen to him. He wanted to throw her across her bed and devour her! He did neither. Instead he returned to the family room to sit in the dark and work on a plan to get Val to stay.

Val woke at the crack of dawn on Christmas day. Dread had formed a heavy ball in the pit of her stomach. Could she say she was sick and stay home in bed all day? No...as much as she wanted to leave, she didn't want to miss any precious time with Jess...and yes, with George, too. These would be the last memories she had of them and that they had of her. She had to make the best of them. So with a soft grunt, she rolled out of bed and began getting ready for Christmas with the Richards family.

A few hours later, as George was packing the minivan with all their gifts, Val gathered the desserts that she and Jess had made. Cookies, cake, pie...they had done it all and she could only hope that it would feed forgiveness from the Richards family.

When everything was packed into the van, George herded his daughter out the front door, leaving Val to lock up.

"I can't wait to see what Santa left for me at Nana and Paw-Paw's," Jess said from the back seat.

"Christmas is more then getting gifts from Santa, little bit," George admonished.

"Yes, Daddy," her voice was contrite but the excited sparkle was still in her eyes.

Val sat silently, trying not to assert herself into their conversation. The sooner she faded away, the better.

"Do you think Nana will like the picture frame I made her?" Jess asked to no one in particular.

"Of course she will!" George reassured her. "She loves everything you make for her."

"Val, did you used to make things for your Nana?" Jess wanted to know.

"I never knew my Nana or Paw-Paw."

"Why not?"

Val tried not to look over to George for support. "They died before I was born."

"And they never came back?"

"Jess, remember how we talked about the hamster at school?" George asked. "He died one night and went to heaven."

"Yeah."

"That's what happened to Val's grandparents. They went to

heaven," he told her carefully.

They all lapsed into silence and shortly thereafter, Jess fell asleep.

"Val."

She looked up at the sound of her name. George was looking at the road but focusing on her. "Yes?"

"I'm sorry if I hurt you," he said softly. "I know you feel rejected after what happened in the kitchen that night..."

"Don't," she interrupted, not wanting him to start listing how different she was from Bernice. "You don't need to say anything else."

"Yes, I do." He wanted her to know that the problem was with him, not her. "I need you to understand what happened."

"No!" she cried, then looked guiltily over her shoulder to see if she had woken Jess. "I mean, please, just let it go."

"But it wasn't about you, Val," he tried to explain.

"George, stop. I told you that you don't owe me anything." She ended the conversation by crossing her arms and looking out the side window.

He gripped the steering wheel so tightly that his knuckles turned white. She was being so unreasonable! What was wrong with her? He was trying to explain, to apologize and she wouldn't even listen. "Valerie," he started angrily.

"Daddy?" Jess interrupted, her voice soft with sleep. "Are you and Val fighting?"

"No, sweets."

"Then why did you say her name like that?" she asked.

"I was trying to get her attention, sweets," he lied.

"You only say my name like that when I've been bad. Was Val bad?"

He groaned at her continuous questions. "No, babe, she wasn't bad. We're almost to Nana's now, okay?"

"Okay, Daddy. Just don't be mad on Christmas," she told him. "Promise?"

Letting out a whoosh of air, he nodded, "I promise." With a sidelong glance at Val, he returned his concentration to the road. About five minutes later, he pulled into the Richards' driveway.

Val let herself out of the car, then turned to help Jess out of her safety seat.

"Jess, come grab some gifts," George ordered from the rear of the minivan.

Val followed her and reached for the tin of cookies. The minute Jess bounded away with her own packages, George grabbed her arm. She froze, but did not meet his gaze.

"This is not over," he whispered fiercely. "I will not let you run off without letting me explain myself to you."

She didn't respond, only slid her arm from his grasp and walked away with food piled up in her arms. Marcy met her at the door and relieved her of a cake plate.

"You do realize that Ed has been waiting for you all morning," Marcy teased her. When Val's response was only a small smile, she frowned. One look at her son's face a few minutes later confirmed her suspicions. Something was wrong.

"Hi, Mom," he greeted her with a hug and a kiss. When he pulled away, she raised her eyebrows at him. "Where's Dad?"

"He's in the living room, watering the tree," she responded. "Why don't you just put your gifts in there for after lunch."

"Good idea."

Val excused herself and disappeared into the powder room. With the door firmly closed and locked, she let her body tremble in reaction to George's words. She wanted nothing more than to escape...why was he doing this to her? He didn't want her, why was he rubbing it in? Why was he prolonging her agony? She splashed some water on her face, then went to join everyone in the living room.

"Val! My cake goddess," Ed greeted her with a big hug. "I'm so glad you're here."

"Hi, Ed," she responded. "Hope you're hungry."

"I didn't eat all day yesterday in preparation," he said smoothly, then shushed his wife when she tried to snitch on him.

"Have you heard from Erik and Robyn already?" George asked from his position on the couch.

"Yes, they called after breakfast," Marcy said, hugging Jess in her arms. "Robyn is a little tired, but her doctor says she's doing fine. They'll be here next week to celebrate New Year's with us."

George hadn't heard about Erik and Robyn's New Year's plans until now. His eyes found Val's face but she refused to meet his gaze. So that was how she planned to get away. Well, he wasn't going to let that happen. Maybe he could convince his brother to change his plans.

"George, why don't you come help me in the kitchen for a moment? Then, maybe if Jess is good, we can open one gift before supper," Marcy said.

George sighed and followed his mother into the kitchen. He was barely in the room when she grabbed his arm and dragged him to the farthest end of the room.

"What's going on?"

"It's just a misunderstanding," he told her. "We'll work it out."

She frowned and released him. "I'm not going to ask you what happened because it's none of my business. But I am going to advise you to be honest with her."

"Mom?" he called her as she turned toward the oven.

"Yes?"

"Bernice called me."

She turned back to him, her face registering shock. "What?!"

"She called and asked for a picture of Jess," he said quietly. "I couldn't believe it."

Marcy shook her head. "What did you tell her?"

"I said no. I don't want her reappearing every couple of years to threaten Jess' happiness. I told her to contact my lawyer if she had any other questions."

"Oh, George," she sighed. "I feel so sorry for that girl. She had no idea what she was getting herself into."

"But I can't just let her in whenever the mood strikes her," he protested. "Who knows if she'd stay or walk away again."

"I understand, but I still feel sorry for her. She was too young," Marcy tsked quietly.

Chapter
Thirteen

The van was once again packed with gifts and Val was waiting for George to finish saying his good byes. Then it was her turn for hugs.

"We're so glad you were with us." Ed hugged her and bussed her cheek. "Come back anytime, doll. With or without cake."

She smiled. "Thank you for inviting me. I know Christmas is usually a family holiday."

"You *are* family, Valerie," Marcy said as she pulled Val into her arms. "And we appreciate you for more than your baking skills." As she hugged Val, she leaned close to her ear and whispered, "Don't let him drive you off. He's only a man, after all."

Val closed her eyes against the tears and gave Marcy one last squeeze before stepping back. How she missed having that kind of closeness with her own mother. "Good night."

"See you in a couple of days," George called, ushering his daughter out to their car.

Following them, Val kept her distance. She was way too attached to these people. Leaving them was going to break her heart into tiny little pieces. Not waiting for George to finish helping Jess, she pulled open the front door and slid into the bucket seat. Thirty minutes and she would be able to hide away in her room. If she could only avoid any further conversations with George.

George sat in the driver's seat and pushed the key into the ignition. The silence in the car seemed almost deafening. Out of the corner of his eye, he could see Val staring out her window. She had done her damnedest to not speak to him all day and it looked like she expected to continue the trend. Well, she could sit there, all smug and silent but he was going to speak with her before the night was through. He would break through her wall and he would have his say.

"Daddy?"

"Yes, sweets?"

"Why didn't Santa bring me a dog?" her voice was heavy with exhaustion.

"Maybe Santa didn't think you were ready to care for a dog," he answered patiently.

"But I was a good girl! And I asked him for a dog."

"I know you did, babe. Maybe next year."

She sniffled loudly, then began crying in earnest.

Val scooted into the back seat and tried to soothe the tired child. "I'm sorry you were disappointed, Jess." She reached over the back seat to find the stuffed dog she'd bought for Jess. "Why don't you hold onto this puppy for me?"

Jess stuck her thumb into her mouth and grabbed the plush toy with her other hand.

"Close your eyes, baby, and we'll be home before you know it," she whispered.

George glanced up in his rear view mirror and his throat tightened. How was he going to survive without her? She was as much a part of his life as his own family. He could not let her go. He could see her stroking his daughter's hair, caring for her as if she had borne her. How could she possibly leave them? If he didn't know better, he'd be thinking that all women could just abandon their children. But no, his own mother had been devoted to her family one hundred percent.

But Val's life had been transient...did she think all families survived like that? Just move on when things got a little too tough? By the time he pulled into his driveway, Jess was sound asleep.

"I'll take her upstairs while you unpack the car," Val murmured without looking up. She was out the sliding door and unhooking Jess before he had turned off the van's engine. It took her just a minute to cradle the sleeping child in her arms and stride quickly to the front door.

George watched them go, his heart sinking as Val disappeared through the front door. He had a feeling he would not see her again that night. Could this Christmas get any worse? He unloaded the car alone, stacking the gifts in the family room where they could go through them tomorrow. As usual, his parents had spoiled Jess rotten, buying her more clothes and toys than she could ever use. And still, with all her gifts, she wanted a damn dog. Guilt had pierced his heart at her sobs of disappointment.

Grunting, he closed up the van and then locked the front door behind him. He glanced quickly at the answering machine in the kitchen, not expecting to see he had a message. Maybe they had forgotten something at his parents'. As he listened to the message, he frowned. The man's voice was unfamiliar, but his name was not. It was Bernice's father, asking him to call back, no matter what the time was. It was a strange call, as he'd never actually spoken to either of her parents before.

He contemplated, for just a moment, putting off the call to Bernice's father until tomorrow. But the man had requested a return call that evening, no matter what the time. Picking up the phone, he made the call.

"Hello?"

The voice that answered the phone was rough. "Mr. Callahan? This is George Richards returning your call."

"Yes," he cleared his throat. "Thank you for calling us back. We, uh," his voice broke.

George froze, his throat closing up.

"I'm sorry to call you on Christmas day...," Mr. Callahan continued. "But I felt it was important that you know."

"Bernice?" George choked.

"She was in an accident...she died immediately."

Closing his eyes, George tried to focus. After a moment, he nearly fell onto a kitchen chair. "What happened?"

"She hadn't been well...she'd taken to drinking and that killed her common sense. She...she just hadn't been well."

George could hear her slightly slurred voice, begging him for a picture. He'd assumed it was tears altering her voice, now he wasn't so sure. "I am so sorry for your loss, Mr. Callahan."

"She was a good girl...but she'd had problems with depression all her life. Did you know that? She was so beautiful and had so many friends...her mother and I could never understand."

"I am so sorry," George repeated.

"She loved you and she loved that baby. She just never could get control of her problems," he continued. "We stayed away from you and the baby for Bernice's sake. We hope that someday you'll allow Mother and myself to be a part of that little girl's life."

"I think that would be wonderful for Jess to know her mother's family," George said softly.

"Jess," he whispered.

"Jessica."

"Jessica," Mr. Callahan paused, "we're not having a service for Bernice; we're just cremating her. Perhaps in a few weeks we can call you again about seeing the baby...Jessica?"

"Of course. I'll be expecting to hear from you."

"Thank you, George."

"Thank you for letting me know about Bernice. I know this was hard for you," George told him before saying good bye. Then he sat in the dark, silent kitchen, trying to absorb the news. His bright and beautiful ex-wife, whom he'd fallen for because of her vivaciousness...she had suffered from depression? How could he have missed that? She'd never been much of a social drinker with him...granted, most of the time he'd spent with her had been after they discovered her pregnancy.

Dropping his head into his hands, he moaned softly. How was he going to explain this to Jess? How much did she really need to know right now? Once again, he wished for some kind of manual to help him deal with the small child whose very life and happiness was in his hands.

Val slipped down the hall toward the stairs. George had taken this week off to spend extra time with Jess, so she assumed he was sleeping in this morning. She was at the base of the stairs when she heard her name being called softly from the family room. She froze

134

and considered retreating.

"Val," he called again. "I know you're there."

Shivering at the sound of his voice, she turned and entered the room. He was slumped in the far corner of the couch wearing dark gray sweat pants and a matching sweat shirt. His face was shadowed and unshaven and his eyes looked tired and sunken. Her heart contracted and she wondered if he was sick. Steeling herself, she faced him.

"I need to talk to you."

"There's nothing left to say," she said firmly.

"There's been an accident."

Her stomach dropped at his blunt announcement and she clutched for the back of the recliner. "Who?!" Robyn's face fluttered in front of her eyes, then Erik's and Maddie's.

He didn't look up so he missed the stricken look on her face. "Bernice. She's dead."

Relief poured through her and then shame. Bernice had been a human being, even if she hadn't been a good parent. Val refocused her gaze on George, wondering how he would deal with this blow to his newly reformed relationship with his ex.

"So you understand when I ask you to stay," he continued.

She frowned and straightened. "Excuse me?"

"This is going to be very difficult for Jess to understand and she's going to need your support and stability," he explained. "We need you to stay."

Jess didn't even know her mother so how much would this loss really affect her? No, George wanted her to stay for *his* sake. The woman he really wanted was gone so he was going to return to his second choice. No way...she had always been second, or even third best as a foster child...she would not stand for it any longer. She wanted to be cherished, to be number one in someone's life. "No, I can't stay."

He frowned and sat forward on the couch. "You mean you won't stay."

Shrugging, she crossed her arms over her chest, protecting herself from the hurt in his voice.

"How can you desert that little girl?" he snarled at her. "How can you just walk away?"

Already he was confusing her with Bernice. "I think those are things you should have asked Bernice. When you're ready to tell Jess about the death of her absentee mother, let me know and I'll be available to help her deal with it. But I am leaving in a week."

"You have no sense of loyalty...no commitment," he accused.

She straightened to her full height, which wasn't much, and glared at him. "Don't throw your guilt on me. You're the one who let Bernice walk away from you and her daughter. You're the reason Jess is going to grow up without a mother," she hissed before turning and practically running from the room. She was not good at confrontations and she absolutely hated hurting someone she loved. With a soft hiccup, she bounded up the stairs and into the privacy of her bedroom. It was there that she let the sobs come. She cried for the little girl she loved...Jess would never get the chance to know her mother. She cried for the little girl she used to be...she too had to live with the understanding that her own mother was gone forever. She cried because she knew how Jess would feel as a grown woman who never knew her mother.

George chose to tell Jess about Bernice right away. He didn't bother to ask Val to join them for the conversation...he was too angry with her because of her accusations.

"Jess, I need to tell you something," he sat down with her in the family room later that morning.

She settled easily on his lap. "Yes, Daddy?"

He inhaled the sweet smell of childhood innocence. This announcement would inevitably change her life. "We need to talk about something very sad."

She wrinkled her nose at him. "Are you sad?"

"Yes, sweets, I am sad," he murmured, pulling her closer to him. "It's about your mommy."

"I don't know who my mommy is," she said simply.

"I know, sweets. She was not able to take care of you so she made me promise to love you and care for you by myself." He ran a hand along her soft blond hair. "And then Jenny came to help us...and then Val," his voice broke on her name. "So you've had a lot of nice people taking care of you."

"I love Jenny and Val."

"I had hoped that one day you would meet your mommy and learn to love her, too," he murmured softly. "But she got sick...and unfortunately, baby, she went to heaven."

"Like Val's Nana and Paw-Paw?" she asked curiously.

"Yes, just like Val's grandparents."

"Why did she die?"

"Because she was sick," he answered patiently.

"So if I get sick, I'll die too?"

"No! Not everyone who gets sick will die," he soothed her. "But your mommy was one of the people who did."

"I don't understand, Daddy."

"I'm not sure I do, either. But I do know that your mommy was a good person and she loved you very much," he hugged her tightly. "And now you have an angel in heaven looking out for you."

Val covered her mouth with her hand and shrank back into the shadows on the staircase. He had been more than kind to Bernice's memory. How lucky Jess was to have a father to love her and anchor her. She'll do just fine after Val's departure.

He only had a few days left with Val in his life so George knew he had to do a few things really quickly. Over dinner that night, he announced that he had to leave town for a day. He politely asked Val to watch Jess for the day since he would be leaving the house early and returning late.

When he left the house the next day, he had a ball of dread in the pit of his stomach. He really did not want to make this trip, but it was something he felt he needed to do...both for Jess and for Bernice.

Later that night, he returned with a small suitcase that he took directly into his bedroom. There he began unpacking the items onto his bed. Bernice's parents had been generous, sending dozens of pictures and even some of Bernice's favorite items to be put away for Jess. They had been thrilled to accept the packet of photos he'd put together in return. So here he was, at eleven p.m., sorting through pictures of Bernice's life to pass along to his daughter.

Bernie had been a beautiful child, similar in stature and shape to Jess. He wondered if Jess would ever have to struggle with depression...if it was an inherited trait. He would need to do some research for her future.

Sifting through more things, he found one of her diaries as well as some pictures she'd sketched. Who knew she'd had some artistic talent? The more he looked through her belongings, the more he realized that he hadn't known anything about her. He had only begun to scratch the surface with his visit today and hoped that Bernice's parents would continue to educate Jess about her mother's life.

Had he always been like this? Taking only what he wanted from the women he dated? Not asking to know her any more than it was necessary to carry on a normal conversation? And had he kept himself closed off from those women? He'd always felt that he'd been a perfect gentleman...chivalrous and kind. He'd talked about himself and his family, but only superficially...he'd assumed other people wouldn't care to know much more.

Exhausted, he put Bernie's things aside, stripped down to his boxers and fell into bed.

Passing by George's empty room the next morning, Val spotted an open suitcase peeking around the end of the bed on the floor, several items still scattered around it. After George's mysterious disappearance yesterday, she was unable to stop herself from tiptoeing into the room to get a closer look. As she came almost on top of the case, she began to realize that there were pictures and papers and books on the floor, with more things still inside the case. Squatting down she found a picture of a young woman who looked exactly like Jess, but maybe ten years older. With a startled gasp, Val dropped the picture like it had scorched her hand. These were mementos of Bernice! So now he was mooning over her even in death? Pain swept through her as she placed her palms on her thighs to push herself upright again. Did she need any *more* proof rubbed in her face? Heart stuttering, she turned and left the room just as she had found it, as if she had never been there at all.

"Just let me talk to him," Robyn whispered several days later. She and Erik has dropped Maddie off at Erik's parents' house, then came to spend time with Val and George on New Year's eve day.

"No." Val folded another shirt and placed it neatly in her suitcase.

"I just want to go."

"Then let Erik talk to him. I know it was a misunderstanding," Robyn pleaded. "George would never go back with Bernie."

"Robyn, I don't want to spend my life competing with a ghost. I will never measure up," she laughed harshly. "I was a handy diversion for George...but obviously I'm not his type and I won't settle for anything less."

"Val! I've seen the way he looks at you. You're important to him."

"Yeah, I take care of his kid and I cook his meals. Of course I'm important to him...who would want to lose that?" she said wryly, folding a pair of pants. "Which reminds me, I'm going to need to pack up my kitchen stuff."

Robyn plopped down onto the bed and watched her friend bustle about the small bedroom. As much as she wanted Val to come back to Maryland, she knew it would be a mistake. George loved her, she just knew it. How was she going to get Val to listen to him? As she sat silently, Val continued to clean out her closet.

"Quit staring at me like that," Val huffed.

"Why would you even think George and Bernice were getting back together?"

"I heard George on the phone with her." Val was too embarrassed to recount what had happened in the kitchen. "I'm not making this up!"

"I never said you were!" Robyn told her. "What did he say when you asked him about the call?"

Val clamped her lips together and swung away.

"You didn't ask him about the call?" Robyn was astonished. "Are you kidding me?"

"I don't need the man to reject me to my face. I'm quite familiar with what rejection looks like." Closing her eyes, she saw his face as he pulled away from her in the kitchen. "He made himself perfectly clear to me. I am not the woman he really wants. I mean honestly," she continued. "Why would he want me after having someone as perfect and beautiful as Bernice?"

Robyn rolled her eyes. "You're a beautiful woman, Val."

"I'm short and round," she mumbled crossly. "George is a great-looking man and he can have any woman he wants."

"Don't make me get up and bop you on the head," Robyn threatened. "George would be lucky to have a woman like you."

"Too bad he doesn't really want me..."

"George!"

He snapped his head up to meet his brother's gaze. "What?"

"You aren't even listening to me," Erik accused.

"Sorry," George muttered, running a hand through his already disheveled hair. "I just know she's up there packing her stuff."

"Since you brought it up, why *is* she packing her stuff?"

"I think she thinks I don't want her in my life."

"And why is that?" Erik asked before taking a sip of his black coffee.

"Because she won't listen to me," George said angrily. "I keep trying to talk to her but she just shuts me out."

"Last time we saw you guys, everything was fine. What happened?"

Glaring at his brother, George tried not to blush. "I kind of attacked her."

"What?!"

George groaned. "Would you keep your voice down, please?"

"What in the hell do you mean you attacked her?" All his protective instincts had Erik's hackles rising.

"Her ex taunted me with their sexual escapades...I didn't want her to think I was boring," he hissed through his teeth. "Do you know that I've never made love outside the bedroom? Other than once on a couch...so we were here in the kitchen and she was just so alluring. I thought I could do it...I thought I could sweep her away."

"And?"

"I couldn't do it. It felt wrong and disrespectful to her as a woman. When I pulled away and saw the hurt in her eyes, I knew it was bad. But hell, I was embarrassed at my behavior."

Erik frowned. "What did you tell her?"

"She won't give me a chance to explain."

"You haven't told her? Jeez, George, and you thought I was bad..."

They were interrupted by a loud screech from upstairs.

The hair on the back of George's neck stood straight up. He was out of his chair in an instant, with Erik right at his heels. As he topped the stairs, he could hear female voices raised in alarm.

"Robyn!" Erik called frantically, terrified that something had happened to her or the baby.

She rushed out of Jess' bedroom, her face white with fear. "Call an ambulance! Call an ambulance!"

George streaked past her, his heart pounding furiously in his chest. "Jess!" He came to an abrupt halt when he spotted Val on her knees hovering over a very still Jess. "Oh, God."

"George, don't!" Val placed her body between him and the prone child. "Don't touch her."

"What happened?!" he ground out, his eyes fixed on his daughter, his heart aching to scoop her into his arms.

"We think she hit her head on the dresser, but we aren't sure," Val whispered. "We can't move her...it's not safe."

He groaned at the sight of the blood matting her hair.

"Don't panic, George. Head wounds always bleed a lot," Val reassured him, her upper body curved protectively over Jess, her hands hovering just above her limbs. It was only a few minutes later when the paramedics appeared in the doorway. Val moved out of their way, then slumped against the wall as they went about their jobs. Her heart still had not returned to its normal pace...hearing that frightened shriek and then seeing Jess on the floor had scared her to death.

George watched in horror as they placed a neck brace around Jess, then carefully rolled her onto a back board. Through all of this, her eyes remained closed and no sound came from her slack lips.

"Which of you are the parents?" a paramedic asked as they were pushing the gurney into the hallway.

"We are," George stepped forward, pulling Val after him.

Val looked up at him in surprise, but let him drag her along the hall and down the stairs.

"We're right behind you," Erik called as his brother and Val disappeared out the front door.

George barely heard him. He hadn't taken his eyes off his daughter for one minute and didn't intend to do so until she opened her eyes and called for him.

Outside, Val hung back as much as George's arm allowed. She wasn't family...there was no way she was going to climb in that ambulance with George.

"Ma'am?" the paramedic inside the ambulance held out his hand to help her inside.

George jerked her forward and handed her up into the truck. With a soft grunt, he followed and settled next to her on the bench. Reaching out, he clutched Val's hand tightly in his and kept his gaze focused on Jess' pale face.

Val gulped and hung on to his hand as the paramedic continued monitoring Jess' condition.

George moaned in anguish as the paramedics disappeared behind the emergency room doors. How was he supposed to protect his baby if they made him stay out here?

"They're taking care of her, George," Val whispered reassuringly. "They can't do that if you're in their way."

He just groaned and continued to peer through the small windows in the doors.

"C'mon, we need to move out of the way." She tugged on his arm to draw him away from the main pathway. As they were nearing the plastic chairs in the waiting room, Erik and Robyn rushed in.

Robyn hugged George, "She'll be fine. I'm sure it was just a knock on the head. Kids are tougher than you think."

"I called Mom. She said she dropped you on your head plenty of times and you turned out okay," Erik joked lamely.

George couldn't concentrate on anything they were saying. He could see their lips moving but his head seemed to be stuffed with cotton so he couldn't hear a word.

"Sit," Val pushed him down onto a chair and sat down next to him. "She's going to be all right, George."

"She's so small," he murmured, letting Val grasp his hand. "And she'll be frightened if she wakes up surrounded by strangers."

"They'll comfort her until someone gets you. They won't let her be scared," Robyn added.

He swallowed and tried not to lose his lunch. What would he do if he lost her? His life would be over.

"Don't, George," Val whispered squeezing his hand. "Don't imagine the worst."

He looked over at her, at the compassion and love that was shining from her eyes. Grabbing her face in his hands, he leaned in so that their noses were almost touching. "Marry me, Val," he whispered fiercely.

Chapter
Fourteen

Her eyes widened in surprise and her mouth dropped open. Behind her, she could hear Robyn making little choking noises. "George..."

"Mr. Richards?"

His eyes flew from Val's to the doctor standing about ten feet away. He dropped his hands and jumped to his feet. "Yes? Yes?"

Val kept herself planted on her chair, even though she wanted to be by George's side to support him. Her heart was pounding hard in her chest both from fear and exhilaration.

"Your daughter is still unconscious but we've stopped the bleeding. It looks like she has a concussion and we would like to get a cat scan to make sure there isn't any swelling in her head," the doctor said calmly. "That's a common test we run when the patient has had a prolonged loss of consciousness. Her vital signs are stable so we're sending her down for the test right now."

"Can I see her?" George whispered, his eyes bright with fear for his only child.

"I'll have the nurse come and get you and your wife as soon as they come back from radiology," the doctor responded before moving away and then out of sight.

George slumped back into his chair and buried his face in his hands. Unconscious...swelling in her head?! His poor baby...

"George..." Val placed a comforting hand on his back. "She's a healthy little girl and tough as nails. She's going to be all right."

Erik disappeared to call Marcy and Ed to update them on Jess' condition. It wasn't much news, but it was more than they knew at the house.

"I can't lose her," George whispered into his hands. "She's my whole world."

Tears pooled up in Val's eyes and spilled over onto her cheeks. She understood...she knew about loss...it was the reason she panicked when people got too close. With a start, she realized that the unbidden thought was true. She was afraid that she would get attached to George and Jess and then he would realize that he didn't love her...then he, too, would leave her. If she were worth loving, her parents would still be alive and Craig would never have left her. Deep down in her child's heart, that was what she truly believed.

"Val," George called her name softly. "Please say you'll stay with me...with us."

She knew the corners of her mouth turned down. "You need to focus on Jess right now, George."

"Together we can take care of her," he told her. "I want us to be together."

Val stood. "Let me go get you some coffee."

"Val..."

"I'll go with you," Robyn said quickly, following Val out of the waiting area. She caught up with Val just down the hall. "Hey..."

"He doesn't love me," Val said defensively.

"He wants to marry you, Val," Robyn corrected.

"He doesn't want to be alone anymore. He can't have Bernice so he's settling for me."

"He never wanted Bernice."

"He's panicked over Jess...he was just looking for something stable to cling to." They reached the lounge area where Val started pouring cups of coffee. "He doesn't love me," she repeated sadly.

George groaned and smacked himself in the head. "What did I do?"

Erik moved to the now empty chair next to his brother. "Did you not mean to propose? Because you kind of did it twice."

"I can't lose them...not either of them. Life without them would be in black and white...," he mumbled. "But blurting out a proposal like that, what was I thinking?"

"It was a bit less than polished," Erik agreed.

146

"And she didn't seem entirely receptive, did she?"

"Uh..."

"Yeah, I know." Standing, George paced along the row of dark green chairs. "Dammit, I can't take this waiting! Why didn't they let me stay with her?"

"Because you're not exactly stable at the moment," Robyn announced as she and Val re-entered the room. She approached her husband and handed him a cup of coffee.

"Mr. Richards?" A petite nurse approached the group.

George whirled around. "Yes?"

"I'm Linda and I'm here to take you in to see your daughter," she smiled warmly.

"Is she all right? Is she awake?" he blurted.

"She's not awake yet, so lets get you and your wife in there to see her, okay?"

Val quickly tucked her hands into her pockets, hoping that George would not be able to grab her. No luck...he wrapped a big hand around her arm and pulled her along with him.

"What did the cat scan show?" he asked Linda.

"I don't know. The radiologist has to look at it then send it up to the doctor. But your daughter's vital signs are still stable and that's a good sign." She led George and Val down the hall into a large room filled with beds, children and beeping machines.

Val gasped and clutched at George's arm. The overwhelming aura of fear and sorrow in the room nearly choked her.

"Jessica is here," Linda said, approaching a bed and nodding to one of the floor nurses monitoring the child in the next bed.

"Jess," George breathed, breaking away from Val and rushing up to the bed. "Oh, baby," he whispered brokenly. Her face and lips were pale, her eyelids crisscrossed with tiny blue veins.

Val closed her eyes briefly before stepping up to the side of the bed next to George. She smoothed a hand along Jess' arm, then wrapped her fingers around Jess' tiny hand. "Hi, sweets. Daddy and I are right here. You're safe now."

Laying a hand on Jess' blond head, George leaned over and kissed her cheek. "Time to wake up, sleepy head," he murmured against her cheek.

"Ten minutes," Linda said quietly before leaving them.

"No way are they taking me away from her again," he said fiercely.

Val continued to stroke Jess' hand, her shoulder brushing against George's. "She's going to be all right." They stood in silence until Linda came back to usher them out.

"No, I don't want to leave her," George hissed.

"I'm sorry, Mr. Richards, but we have rules," Linda said firmly.

"She's my baby, I can't leave her alone."

"George..." Val touched his arm as he stood sentry at the head of Jess' bed.

"Daddy?"

His entire demeanor changed as he turned to lean over his daughter. "Hi there, little bit."

"I'm scared," she whispered. "Don't leave me."

"I'm right here," he reassured her, tears clogging his throat.

Linda pressed the call button and asked for the doctor.

Val circled around the bed to smooth her hand along Jess' hair. "I can't tell you how wonderful it is to see your beautiful blue eyes, Jess."

Jess turned those blue eyes on her father. "Daddy...can I go home now, please? I don't like it here."

The doctor walked in just as Jess made her declaration. "Well, little lady, you have to stay for the night, that's for sure."

Val moved out of the way so the doctor could approach Jess' side. "George," she got his attention. "I'm going to find Erik and Robyn."

He nodded and refocused his attention on soothing Jess while the doctor checked her over.

Val gave them one last look before hurrying down the hall to the waiting room. There she found Erik and Robyn huddled together on a plastic couch. A wave of envy at her best friend's life washed over her. Her step slowed as her heart contracted in pain...would she ever have that? Could she ever trust herself to love like that again?

148

At that moment, Robyn looked up to meet her gaze. "Val?"

"She's awake," Val announced. "The doctor is in with her now."

"Oh thank goodness!" Robyn exclaimed, hugging Erik. "I just knew she would be all right."

Erik hugged her back, then stood and left to call his parents with the news.

Val sank down into the chair next to her best friend. "I am so overwhelmed, Robyn."

Rubbing a hand over her swollen tummy, Robyn asked, "Why?"

"He wouldn't leave her side. Once he got his eyes on her again, that was it," Val whispered.

"Why does that surprise you? Jess is his child."

"No one ever looked at me that way."

Robyn took her best friend's hand in between hers. "That's where you're wrong, Val. I think you just don't see it."

Shaking her head, Val stood and stepped away from Robyn, distancing herself. "You're just too nice to believe something like this...but no one has ever viewed me that way. Not my parents, not one of the many foster families I had...not even Craig."

"Honey, I am positive that your parents loved you desperately."

"Then why did they leave?" Val covered her face with her hands, trying to hide her tears.

Robyn stood and pulled Val into her arms. "They would never have left you if they had been given the choice, honey."

"If they loved me, why didn't they take me with them when they left the house?" came the whispered question.

"Where were they going?" Robyn asked.

"I don't know," Val hiccuped and pulled away to wipe her face. "But I was just a baby...how could they leave me behind?"

"Val, if they hadn't, you'd be dead, too."

Swinging away, Val refused to meet her friend's gaze.

"Maybe you need to find out what really happened," Robyn suggested quietly. "There must be some record somewhere."

"Sometimes I think I'm asking for too much, Robyn," her voice wobbled with emotion. "And then there are the times when I think

I'm just asking for the impossible."

George didn't let go of Jess' hand for the next twenty four hours. He only barely noted the comings and goings of his brother and sister-in-law, though he was clearly aware of Val's presence in the room.

Jess slept a lot over the twenty four hours, her forehead smooth with the knowledge that her father was watching over her.

Val watched all of this while her heart cracked into pieces at the thought of leaving them. She loved them both so desperately...but she could not stay and fight Bernice's ghost for George's affections. She would never know if he was seeing her or seeing Bernice.

"Val?"

She looked up at the sound of her name. Jess was still asleep and George was looking at her expectantly. "Yes?"

"Thank you for staying with me...with us," he said softly.

Her lips flattened. "Nothing has changed, George. Jess is going to be fine and I'm going back to Maryland with Robyn and Erik."

"Why? I know you think I was out of my mind yesterday, but I was serious. I want to marry you."

She swallowed carefully, then hardened her voice. "I don't want to marry you."

His eyes went flat. "I see."

"I would have waited to have this conversation with you until Jess was home, safe and sound," she continued unemotionally. There was no way she could make it through this if she allowed any feelings to creep through her facade.

"How thoughtful of you," he turned his back on her, his attention refocused on his beloved child.

Standing, she crossed her arms over her chest. "I should go." When he didn't respond, she ducked her head and slipped from the room.

It was best, George thought, he needed all his energies for Jess right now. Closing his eyes, he let his head drop forward...she would be gone soon and his life would go on. Before he realized it, tears began streaming down his face. Damn her, he loved her and she just walked away! Was he not enough for any woman? Was he destined to stand by and watch them all walk out of his life?

Val moved out of George's house before he and Jess came home from the hospital on New Year's day. She checked into a nearby hotel to wait for Robyn and Erik to make their trip home. She refused to go to Marcy and Ed's for a celebration dinner for Jess' coming home, but spoke briefly to Jess on the phone. She was able to hold back her tears while speaking on the phone with the little girl, but burst into tears as soon as they hung up. This was nothing like her aborted marriage with Craig...with that, she'd been more angry and confused than hurt. With George and Jess, it was like someone was ripping her heart out of her chest while it was still beating. Even knowing that George didn't love her was not enough to staunch the flow of pain through her body.

When Robyn called later to say she and Erik were extending their stay, Val could find no good way to ask them to change their minds. Instead, she simply called a car rental agency and rented a small car to be delivered to the hotel the next day. She couldn't stay in her hotel room any longer, inactive and miserable.

George sat on the edge of Jess' pink bed and smoothed her fine blond hair off her forehead.

"Daddy, when is Val coming back? I miss her," she whispered sleepily.

He frowned, knowing Jess' stamina had not yet returned. His heart ached for her loss of a friend. "I don't know, baby."

"Did she leave because of my accident?"

"Of course not!"

"Doesn't she love me anymore? If I promise to be good, will she come back?" Tears trickled down her pale cheeks.

"You know she loves you...didn't she tell you that on the phone?"

"Then why, Daddy? Why did she leave? Why did you let her go?" her tears turned into exhausted sobs as she burrowed into his chest. "Make her come back, Daddy!" she wailed.

RIDA ALLEN

Holding her close, he wanted to run out and do her bidding...he wanted nothing more than to go out, grab Val by the hair and drag her back home where she belonged. With a start, he realized what he had just thought...why should he let her walk away? Why shouldn't he fight for what he wanted?

It was too late to go out tonight, but Val couldn't go far...after all, Robyn and Erik weren't leaving for another three or four days.

Checked out? George slammed his fist on the desk top and turned away from the registration desk. It was only ten a.m., where would she have been going this early? Stalking over to the payphone, he called his parents house where he had dropped off Jess only an hour ago.

"Hi, Mom, is Robyn awake yet?" he asked.

"She right here eating breakfast. Hold on," Marcy passed the phone over to her daughter-in-law. "It's George."

"Hi, George," she said around a mouthful of toast.

"Where is she?" he demanded.

"Where is who?"

"Val...where is Val?" he repeated impatiently.

"At the hotel, I assume."

"They said she checked out."

"Oh gosh, I'm sorry, George. She didn't say anything to me last night...maybe she's back at your place?" Robyn suggested hopefully.

"Right...my house," he pursed his lips before barking out a terse good-bye and hanging up. Why would she go back to his house unless...a smile broke out over his face. He loped, almost ran, out to his car and sped back to the house. Bursting through the front door, he called out expectantly, "Valerie!"

The only sound that greeted him was the echo of his own voice. Maybe she was in the bathroom...

He took the stairs two at a time but when he reached the top, he could see the hall bathroom door standing open. Grunting, he strode into his bedroom, but it as well as his bathroom, was empty.

Now what? Where had she gone? He slowly sank down onto the

152

edge of his bed, then stared off into space. The only answer was that somehow, she had left town. Had she called her ex to come retrieve her? How could he respond to that?

It was two weeks and Jess still asked every day when Val was coming home. Robyn, Erik and Maddie had gone home over a week ago, but Robyn swore that she had not seen or spoken to Val since she disappeared. But then again, they all assumed that if Val had returned to Craig, she would be too embarrassed to let Robyn and Erik know.

George finished putting pancakes on Jess' plate, then set it down in front of her.

"Daddy, may I have a banana with my pancakes?" Jess asked.

"Sure, sweets." He peeled a banana, then sliced it onto her plate. "Would you like milk or juice?"

"Juice, please, Daddy," she spoke around a mouthful of food.

And so George continued his daily activities, feeling like he was sleep walking through his life.

"Daddy?"

He turned back to her, "Yes?"

"She'll be back soon."

Frowning, he set her glass of juice on the table, "What?"

"I had a dream last night that Val came home and she brought me a dog," Jess said matter-of-factly before taking a drink of orange juice.

"Jess..."

"It's okay, Daddy...I know the dog part is something I made up. But the part about Val is real," she said confidently.

He sighed and slid onto a chair across from her. "Honey, no one has heard from Val for a couple of weeks."

"I've talked to her," Jess said absently.

"What?!"

"She calls me every morning, Daddy," another whole pancake disappeared into her mouth. "Just like she said she would before she went away. Val says to never say something unless you mean it."

"When does she call you?" He never once heard the phone ring without him answering it.

"She calls when you're in the shower. I wake myself up and wait in her room for her to call me," she explained.

"Where is she?"

Jess shrugged delicately. "She said she's doing very important things. But she always says she loves me before she hangs up. And she never says anything unless she means it."

"Why didn't you tell me about this?"

"Val said it was our special secret. But since she's coming home, I guessed it was okay to tell you." She took another gulp of her juice before hopping off her chair.

'Did she tell you she was coming back here?"

"I told you, Daddy, I dreamed it last night." She kissed his cheek then skipped out of the room.

George watched her go, a mixture of joy and anguish on his face. She really was a wonderful child and he hoped that no matter what, Val would not destroy her.

Val clutched the books against her chest and stood silently in front of a house. Her knees wobbled and her breath caught in her throat, but she pressed the doorbell anyway. A moment later, the door flew open.

"Val?!"

She smiled tentatively and hugged the books closer. "Hi."

"I don't know whether to hug you or slug you!" Robyn cried, then pulled Val into the house. "Where the hell have you been?" She crushed Val against her for a long moment, aware that she was swamped with relief and joy at seeing her best friend.

Val hugged Robyn back, then stepped back and followed her into the family room. "Wait until you hear what I've found out, Robyn."

"Well, come tell me what the heck you've been doing for the past two and a half weeks." Robyn waddled over to the couch and plopped down.

"I did what you suggested, Robyn...I went to find out what

happened when my parents died."

"No!"

"Yes! And I can't believe what I found. Not only was I able to see the police report, but there were hospital files and social services files! Robyn," she leaned forward and dropped her books onto the coffee table. "My parents were on their way to the hospital to have a baby."

"What?!"

"I know, I couldn't believe it either! But it was there in all the reports."

"How old were you?"

"I was two and they left me with an older couple who lived next door. I even found them...they said they knew my parents for about five years before they died. They said my parents absolutely doted on me...that I was spoiled rotten. They said my parents were so excited about having another child." Val's face was shining with joy. "They said I should come back anytime to visit."

"And what about these?" Robyn gestured to the books on the table.

"Photo albums. I'd packed them away years ago. Only after reading all the hospital reports did I go back and actually look through the albums. This one," she pointed to a red one, "was from my birth and up until they died. That one," she gestured toward the navy blue one. "Has pictures of my mom pregnant with my baby brother."

"How do you know it was a boy?"

"I saw his birth certificate, Robyn."

"No!"

"Yes!" She pulled out a copy of the hospital form. "They delivered him by c-section."

"He survived?!"

"Yes!"

"I can't believe this," Robyn breathed.

"As far as I can tell, he became a ward of social services right away. He went into the foster care system before the police even found out about me." She paused to catch her breath. "The Cantors, our neighbors, called the hospital the next day when they didn't hear from Mom or Dad about the delivery. They called the police but they agreed to take care of me while paperwork was being processed over my parents' death. There was no will, no relatives...the Cantors didn't even know about my brother surviving. So our cases stayed separate...and my brother got adopted almost right away."

"And there was no one to tell you about him."

"I'm going to find him, Robyn. He's my family," Val said firmly. "And I know my parents would want us to know each other...to be together."

"This is amazing."

"There are notes in these albums...from my parents to me as a baby. The same in my brother's album. And Mrs. Cantor says that somewhere I must have the baby book she helped my mother make." Finally, Val ran out of breath and sank back against the couch cushions.

"My God, Val, this is so much to take in."

"I know...it's like a whole part of my life has appeared out of the dust."

"They loved you, Val," Robyn said softly, a smile on her face.

"Yeah, I guess they did."

"And they're not the only ones."

Val's smile dimmed a little.

"You have to talk to him..."

"He doesn't love me, Robyn. I won't settle for anything less...especially now."

Robyn shook her head and pushed herself to a standing position. "Don't you move, girl...I need to visit the bathroom before we get any further into this conversation."

Watching her waddle away, Val felt that warm embrace of friendship surround her. No matter what, she was safe here in this home. Robyn was like family and she knew she would get unconditional support in the search for her brother. That, after all, was why she had come.

Val held little Maddie in her lap as they ate dinner. Neither Erik nor Robyn had suggested she call George, though she could see the words in their eyes. Instead they had both hugged her and insisted she say with them as long as she wanted.

She was upstairs tucking Maddie in, thinking of her little brother, when she heard a commotion downstairs. Assuming that the dog had done something wrong, she continued reading Maddie's bedtime story. When the precious toddler finally allowed sleep to overtake her, Val stood and tiptoed from the room. She walked along the darkened hall and down the stairs. As she turned to enter the family room, she heard noises along the back of the house where the den was. Shrugging, she stepped into the family room, then froze.

"Hello, Val."

After a moment of silence, Val snapped her mouth shut and let her eyes devour him. She had missed him so much.

"Nothing to say? That's all right...I have plenty to say to you," George gestured to the couch. "Why don't you sit down?"

She rounded the corner of the sofa, then perched on the edge of the seat cushion.

He remained standing, adrenaline flowing through his body at a fast pace. She was beautiful...her green eyes dark with emotion, her body ripe and womanly just as he remembered. It felt like they had been separated for months rather than weeks. "When Robyn called me to say you'd finally reappeared, I couldn't decide if I was relieved or disappointed."

Hurt pierced her and she tried to steel herself against his words.

"I was relieved to know you were safe, but disappointed to know it wasn't me you wanted to see first," he told her. "But on the drive down here, I thought about it. Why would you come to me when I'd given you no reason to?"

Val didn't know how to respond, so she remained silent.

"I've done a lot of things wrong in my life...I don't want to mess this up, too." He approached the couch, then knelt down in front of her. "Valerie, I love you with every fiber of my being. Please, will you marry me and make me whole?"

She choked as she looked into his beloved face. "George..."

"I know things got messed up along the way, but I was trying to be someone I wasn't...I can only be me and pray I'm what you want," he whispered, holding her hand in his.

"What...what are you talking about?" she asked him in a thready voice.

"That night, in the kitchen when I tore your blouse...I thought that was what you wanted."

"I wanted you to ruin my clothes?" she was totally confused.

"I thought you wanted me to sweep you off your feet...I thought you wanted me to throw you down on the floor and ravage you. But I just can't do those things...I'm just not programmed that way," he murmured. "If you can accept that about me, I'll try to make you happy in other ways."

She pulled away and stood. "George, you sweep me away every time you touch me! You cherished me in a way no one ever has! I never wanted anything more."

"But your ex..."

"Is my *ex*, and for good reasons, George." Shaking her head, she closed her eyes. "That is why you walked away in the middle of making love to me?!"

He got to his feet and grasped her by the shoulders, forcing her to look at him. "What did you think?"

"I thought you were comparing me to Bernice," she whispered. "and found me lacking."

"Oh good lord...all that time?!" he groaned. "Why would you even think of Bernice?"

"Because I heard you talking to her on the phone. I thought you were considering getting back with her before she died," Val explained.

He rested his forehead against hers. "No...she called to ask for pictures of Jess. I told her to speak to my lawyer if she needed to be refreshed on our legal agreement."

"I couldn't stand the thought of being your second choice."

"We're fools. We, who promised to tell each other only the truth, no matter what..." he muttered wryly.

"I'd been lied to so many times, George...I was always afraid that everything I was hearing was a lie. That I wouldn't be able to see the difference."

"Listen to me," he shook her gently. "I love you. I want to marry you. I want you to be with me always. Truths, Val...all truths."

She threw her arms around his neck and kissed him. With a throaty laugh, she pulled him to the floor in front of the couch and began sweeping *him* away.

Neither heard the muffled giggles as the brother and the best friend slipped along the hallway and up the stairs to their own room.

Epilogue

"Let me hold her."

"No, let *me* hold her."

"Be careful, you're squishing her!"

"Am not!"

Robyn rolled her eyes as she rubbed four month old baby Evan's back as he lay against her shoulder.

Laughing, Val watched as Jess and her cousin Maddie argued over the bundle of black fur being passed from embrace to embrace. They had finally given in to Jess' repeated request for a dog companion and gotten her a flat-coated retriever that they aptly named Pandora.

"I knew this would be a zoo," George groaned, settling onto a patio chair next to his soon-to-be bride.

"Oh hush, they're having a good time," Val reprimanded him.

"So finish telling us what you found out," Erik prompted from his chair.

"Well, it seems he was adopted by a Maryland couple," Val told them. "As far as I know, they're still in the area, though I don't know if *he* is."

"What do you do now?" this was from Robyn.

"Register on the databases for families searching for their biological roots...hope that he's looking."

"What about contacting the family directly?"

"I don't want to wreck all their lives," Val responded to Erik's question. "For all I know, they had no idea there was a sibling."

"What if he doesn't know he was adopted?" Robyn again.

George rubbed the back of Val's neck in a comforting gesture. "We're trying to take this one step at a time. We don't want anyone to be hurt in this process."

"Can you check to see if he's registered in one of those

databases?" Erik suggested. "Maybe he's already looking for you?"

"The records show his parents are deceased, so he could find that out easily if he's looked. But they didn't show a sibling...there's no reason to suspect he'd be looking," Val announced unhappily.

"Then there must be something more we can do!" Robyn exclaimed, setting the baby into his carrier to nap.

"I don't know. Maybe I could have a third party contact him to see if he's interested in meeting me. No pressure if it's impersonal, right?"

"I may even know someone through work who can help us," George said thoughtfully. "In fact, I'm sure Jordan would do it."

"Do you know your brother's name, Val?" Robyn's voice was hopeful.

"His name is Jack...Jack Morgan."

Printed in the United States
17191LVS00001B/211

9 781413 708158